ENTHRALLING TRAILS:
A REFLECTION OF LIFE

ENTHRALLING TRAILS: A REFLECTION OF LIFE

JYOTHI RAMESH PAI

PARTRIDGE
A Penguin Random House Company

ISBN: Softcover   978-1-4828-4108-4
             eBook   978-1-4828-4107-7

To order additional copies of this book, contact
Partridge India
000 800 10062 62
orders.india@partridgepublishing.com

www.partridgepublishing.com/india

CONTENTS

This book is a manifestation of thoughts inspired through the motivation I received from my parents.

I dedicate this book to my late parents Shri. A. S. Pai and Mrs. Leela Pai and to My late father in law Shri R. V Rao

PREFACE

Words have the gift to articulate one's feelings. Words as a part of good literature endure with time influencing thoughts and behavior of an individual. Words have the Power to transform the world. Emotions like compassion, love, friendship, honesty, kindness, mercy, politeness and many more are inspirations brought to mind through words. Language is a powerful tool in enthusing feelings among fellow beings. These narratives carry a message in the mundane day to day happenings. These were begun with an intention of including a beautiful person who has influenced my life but it includes a few stories which are a social issue in India. I have always believed that each of us is unique in some way as we may not have everything but everyone of us have something which only another beautiful heart can note.

My research on Sudha Murty's books and her saying that 'life is a vast storehouse of stories' is in someway responsible for the commencement of these narratives. It was a simple thought shared by my son 'Nishant' who taught me the art of beginning a blogger account, penning my thoughts and publishing these in all sincerity. It also taught me that visualization of the world is indeed a reflection of thoughts. The publication every week with the feedbacks received helped me improvise my writings keeping the language simple for readers to enjoy. My friends and family played a great role in its growth. My research on Ruskin Bond's books taught me the magnificence of language and the conviction of loving what one does.

I thank Mr. Ashutosh Madhav Joshi who was pivotal in teaching me the art of simplicity in writings helping me go ahead in this venture. I share my deepest acknowledgments with my friend Durga Chavan for sharing these experiences. I thank all my classmates and friends for their patience and their regularity in reading these narratives. My earnest gratitude to my dear husband Mr. V Ramesh and my mother in law Mrs. Sulochana Ammal who were pillars of support in my good times and hard times making life a beautiful one. I thank all those charismatic human beings in the narratives who lent me their time and experiences making my life a richer one in warmth and understanding. Omissions, if any, are entirely unintentional

1

ETERNAL BLISS

"Meaning does not lie in things. Meaning lies in us."
— Marianne Williamson

A strong nudge made me turn indignantly only to find a little girl looking at me serenely. She was roughly nine years old and had a little boy accompanying her. She was dark with gleaming eyes, wearing a long skirt and blouse, her curly hair left open with an orange mark on her forehead. The boy was younger than her, untidily dressed in a white shirt and colored shorts. They were holding a flat plate with a few idols of Gods and Goddesses in it. I nodded my head in disapproval and moved ahead. It pained me that these little children found pride in begging, and giving them money would turn them into scrupulous vagrants.

They did not mind it, and walked briskly down slope on the mall road in Manali which was filled with tourists who were gay and debonair. We were put up at hotel Kanishka which was just half a km away from mall road in Manali. The mall road has a large central clearing with shops lined on both the sides of a long road. There are paved spherical firmaments and benches designed for tourists and others to sit and watch. We saw a group of localites who danced depicting their customs and traditions in this clearing. The shops were bustling with people. There were eateries, shops selling artifacts, shawls, woollens, toys and many more. It was late in the evening; we could see the Majestic Himalayas from one end. There were hordes of tourists from all over India who had gathered there. There was a masseur who was giving a professional massage to an old lady sitting on a bench in the square.

I noticed a larger crowd at a place. We peered to see people listening to a foreigner who was singing in all reverence. He had a sandalwood mark on his forehead; his fingers moved smoothly on the keys of a harmonium, an Indian lady accompanied him on the Dhol (drum) kept there. It took me a few minutes to grasp that he sang a bhajan (hymn) in Sanskrit. There was an another foreigner, a young lady, dressed in a long skirt and blouse with her hair left loose reminding me of the little vagrant as she came near and showed us some thin small Hindi spiritual books. She said 'give me anything' in Hindi. I walked away unknowingly wondering whether I must appreciate or help.

The day before we started back we asked the driver to take us to Vasisht Kund, a hot water spring which was found by the mythological sage Vashishta. My son tired after the Rohtang pass visit preferred staying back. We reached the place soon. Since the roads were narrow we had to get off the car and begin climbing a steep path. There were shops lined on both the sides of the road leading to the temple, we found that the spring was inside the temple. We had plenty of time on hand so decided to walk ahead to see a waterfall called Yogini waterfalls. It is a 45 minutes trek in the lonely mountain paths. The road past the temple grew narrower and we could see motels and small rooms and tenements closely packed with horses and cows being led to the mountains for grazing. There was a small opening, plastered with cement with a water pipe where I saw men and women washing their clothes. I saw a cow jump into it, to drink water. I looked ahead to reach the waterfalls, we climbed and moved ahead, we found a half built house on a slope.

There was a tent put up in the yard and there were a few more foreigners living in miserable conditions with shrewd Indians serving them. While returning back I observed the place better, a little away from the temple I saw a young foreigner sitting on the bare ground in a room whose doors were thrown open facing the narrow street. He stared into nothingness and seemed to be in a trance. I started rushing back as the warmth of the afternoon sun was now unbearable; perhaps it was the realization which had turned me hot and angry. I began speculating as we travelled back.

They say spirituality is a feeling of contentment and peace, an eminent state of rational awakening, a world of significance where a person rises as a personality with the love of God, and goodness defusing stress, leading one to an everlasting world of bliss. The little girl begging in the market square was aping the foreigners in the path of spirituality as they gained the consideration of the tourists through their sophisticated ways of begging. They were on narcotics and drugs with the money plundered while playing with the sentiments and convictions of people. I came to know that they had these rented places to live because they stayed for months in these places with no one to evict them, their families having written them off. The little girl's resentfulness towards tourists was their refusal to acknowledge her spirituality. Was her adoration for God lesser than the foreigner's?

Is spirituality an escape from our duties, is it just high thinking in a limited world of eternal contentment of self?

"The poverty in the West is a different kind of poverty -- it is not only poverty of loneliness but also of spirituality. There's a hunger for love, as there is a hunger for God." — Mother Teresa

2

A PROMISING TOMORROW

"Being deeply loved by someone gives you strength, while loving someone deeply gives you courage"
— Lao Tzu

I read the article 'Its Hope that keeps us Going' by Eziekel Isaac Malekar. It said that 'Hope' literally means expectation and desire combined. Hope though deceitful carries us pleasantly to the end of life as its hope which keeps us alive.

I read these lines a number of times, each time memories recalled 'him'. He was there for me and my husband whenever we needed money. He was there to comfort us when we felt we had lost each battle in life advising us to not lose hope. He like everyone else had his mood swings. He was tall and well built. He was agile and could keep anyone busy in a conversation or at work. He and my father were friends but poles apart in likes and dislikes. He liked reading, but never wrote. He was an ocean of knowledge who would not spare a person till the person heard the whole story. The last time when I met him he definitely seemed older with a beard and a bent back. He began the conversation, after a while I rushed to the kitchen only to meet him at the threshold. He had taken the second doorway to reach sooner than me. I sighed then, but today they are pleasant memories. I plainly began being friendly only after I lost my father.

Whenever we would go to Kerala he would have a list of recipes ready for me. He would love the food I cooked and compliment it. Each day he would ask me if I needed anything from the market. Going to the market, cycling, talking to people, paying the bills, bringing lot of goodies were a few of the things he would carry on regularly. Many a times I would see him getting the house repaired. He was the one who loved the latest electronic gadgets and the lone one there who would look into the cleanliness of the house he had painfully built. He would describe the pain that inspired a homeless to first build a shelter. He believed in saving but always helped people monetarily especially the ones who yearned to study.

After I lost my father, he would call regularly to speak. Initially, I would end the conversation quickly with the usual greetings but slowly we began speaking about everything in this world. I was learning to drive for the second time. He would motivate me to learn it soon so that I could help my husband while we were on a long drive, perhaps to Kerala. He would definitely ask me what I planned to cook. He would ask me guidelines to make it and end saying that I could cook anything well. He was a food-lover and it was a great compliment for me.

Life went on. One day he informed that he was worried about the regular severe backache he had and that he had been advised for an Ultrasound scan. I could feel the unhappiness in his voice. I told him that it was a procedure followed to know the fact. He bravely went for a sonography which showed a missing vertebra. I wondered when he said that. Was his bone covered by flesh or......... The very next day he was admitted in a hospital and every one of us was informed that there would be a surgery to insert a rod in the weak vertebra so that he could move on for years. A mandatory biopsy was also to be done. He said 'Maybe tuberculosis Jyothi'. I now felt he needed to be hopeful, so said 'may be nothing at all'. He laughed aloud, but the hollowness in his laughter showed there was something missing in it. My husband, his brothers and my mother -in -law were with him during the operation. At 3.30pm, my husband informed me that his vertebral column had turned into a soft pulp like a banana and a few days later that he was declared to be terminally ill with bone cancer. Each one of us resolved not to disclose this to him. He was weak after the operation, but jubilant that the rod would help him back to cycling and lead an active life again. He would talk to me each day informing that he was better. I wondered, but hope does heal people. On the fateful day he was rolled into the Oncology Dept, he understood that he had cancer. He overcame that with the thought that worry and fear were of no avail. He repeatedly encountered patients suffering from cancer to overcome the fear of cancer. He was hopeful that he would recover, but he never knew that the vertebra could never help him stand. He would remain bedridden. My husband took him back home. Within a fortnight, he was very unwell. He would talk to me only if I wanted. Every bit showed that he had lost all hopes. I was attending a workshop at FDRC in Delhi, which made my husband reach Kerala a few days late. He was in a local hospital at Tiruvalla. He was well-looked after, but his back was sore. My husband was informed that he had stopped eating after he came to know that he would be bedridden.

All the signs of hope were now missing. He was fed intravenously against his will. My mother in law said that he had read about mercy killing in Jain philosophy and so felt that it was better to fast unto death rather than live a life of dependency. He spoke inaudibly at 2.30pm and left the world tumbling to death at 4.30pm. His philosophy proved to be a deliverance for him, while his mercy was a deliverance for others who looked after him. Life has startling twists, but man lives on hope but when hope is lost only our good deeds linger pervading the universe.

A tribute to my late father in law Shri. R.V. Rao, who left us on the 27th of September 2010.

3

CAPTIVATED OR INSECURE

"I remember my childhood names for grasses and secret flowers. I remember where a toad may live and what time the birds awaken in the summer -- and what trees and seasons smelled like -- how people looked and walked and smelled even. The memory of odors is very rich." — John Steinbeck, East of Eden

It was dark brown with a white inner; it was long and portly and had curled itself spreading totally on the grill door. The inner wooden door was hanging open. I quickly resolved and shut the wooden door while pulling my son indoors. As we sighed, my husband told me it was a harmless water snake, which must have slithered owing to the heavy rains. I recalled another occasion, when I had seen a viper entwine the hibiscus plant and later spread itself on the roof of the branches not knowing how to escape. I rushed to the terrace and looked down smugly to see it struggle. There I felt a vicious joy surge in as it struggled in despair. I kept looking on as, they say, encountering fear kills fear.

From the first day of our stay in that row house we experienced fear and joy of animals visiting us. The row house had a small backyard which opened into the prohibited area of a three km artificial forest and faced a huge man made lake with pigeons resting all around the trees which lined the lake. The fenced compound wall was lined by huge trees. In summer we had monkeys which would climb up on the terrace wall and terrify with their menacing looks and chatter. I used to keep the doors locked and the glass windows sealed. The kingfisher and other birds would at times screech and make many fearful noises late in the night and early in the morning making me dread thinking that it must have been a cue about the escaped panther or the man eating lion in the jungle. The mornings were exquisite with the chirping of birds, and squeaking of squirrels which would bashfully pick the biscuit kept for it on the parapet wall. Over the years I felt terrorized watching lizards, chameleons, snakes, eagles and crabs, more than ever the huge crab which had walked out of the lake during a lashing rain to crawl up the grill door. It never moved the whole night, but we did not see it in the morning. Gradually I overcame the fear and got friendly with nature and loved being one of them. I never felt the solitude as I was always amongst some animal or the beautiful panorama.

One of those days my husband bought this flat in one of the crowded locales. We wanted a home of our own and moved into this flat. Now when I look out, I can see people around signifying life. The building expands to large vastness with minimum space wasted. The ground has been plastered with cement and the entrance of each area is paved with expensive tiles. There is not a spot wilderness. The plants are fixed in grooves of sand and plastered with cemented surroundings; many a time resemble chained victims. The huge trees in the forest area would sway wildly with wind resembling people but here I found the trees looking frail and sophisticated in their restricted movements like men. There were very few of them. We bought a few plants and began a terrace garden. Still the growth never matches the ones fixed in soil. In the row house it was difficult and required great pains to keep the surroundings clean, leave water for birds and do many more errands while sweeping the surroundings clean, but these cemented locales are easy to clean and look neat.

I see a few crows flying around finding no space to perch, the pigeons building nests in few spaces between the drain pipes or a few neglected window sills adamantly demanding their space. I seemed one amidst nature in the forest area home and here I find wilderness one in the midst of people. There are no animals, no chirping of early morning birds, there's loud noise of the security guard's blowing whistle, but it is safe, very safe but then why do I miss the magnificence of nature, why do I yearn for greenery............... It most certainly reminded me of Gouri Dange's article 'Addicted to concrete' in Pune Mirror newspaper which said

'As of today, we feel threatened by greenery and comforted by cement'.

Jyothi Ramesh Pai

"The planting of a tree, especially one of the long-living hardwood trees, is a gift which you can make to posterity at almost no cost and with almost no trouble, and if the tree takes root it will far outlive the visible effect of any of your other actions, good or evil."
— George Orwell

4

A Frail poise of Life

"No matter the nature of your individuality, you can nurture a better identity and have a mature positively rewarding life." — Ifeanyi Enoch Onuoha

They dragged themselves heaving their luggage till the seat. The boy confirmed the seat numbers. My niece and I moved away so that they were comfortable. I was travelling back to Pune from Hyderabad after visiting my sister who was unwell with a fracture in her ankle. It was painful to see my sister in a troubled state, but ecstatic to meet my siblings and their kids. My niece who was lately married off was also there to take care of her mother. She had come to see me off along with her father.

The man and the young boy huddled in their seats. I had got the window seat in the AC chair car. The train chugged away at sharp 2.45pm. The boy sat next to me and the father a seat away. The whole bogie was filled with people making it very safe for all those who were travelling alone. At the far end was a young woman with a six month old baby. There were youngsters who were probably returning back to their work places after a weekend. It was burning hot at Hyderabad but was very cool and comfortable inside. Travelling by this train is most preferred as it takes the shortest time, helping travellers reach home the same day. The Shatapdi train starts from Pune at 5.50am and reaches Secunderabad at 2.10 pm and starts back at quarter to three to reach Pune at 11.10pm. The train stops at a few major stops as Sholapur, Gulburga, and Tandur. Food and water are supplied and so it relieves the traveler from carrying anything other than the luggage.

The boy was lean and lanky and must have been fifteen to sixteen years old. The father seemed to be from a village but was dressed in a Safari suit, in spite of the hot weather. He seemed uncomfortable and raised a leg and sat with the other leg folded on the seat. The boy listened to songs on the Nokia Mobile. He sporadically kept correcting his father with the vital etiquettes so as to personify themselves as a class apart from what they were. A member of the staff serving at table brought along the tray with snacks, giving time for the passengers to gorge it before serving tea. I had my lunch at my sister's home and did not wish to eat that. I kept reading my book but could hear the boy slowly guide his father to eat. The man ate every thing and did not know what to do with the packet sauce. He asked the boy to pocket it, but the boy asked the father to leave it in the tray. He later opened the plastic pouch containing sugar and milk powder for tea.

The attendant brought cups of hot water and served it; the boy did not want it but was shocked to see that his father had torn the tea packet which had to be dipped in water, spilling the tea leaves in the tray. He slowly whispered in Marathi that the kit was of no use. But the father felt it was hard earned money and put a lot of the spilled leaves in the hot water. With the help of the boy, he added sugar and the milk powder and churned it with a plastic stick vigorously and sipped it loudly. I was watching the child's expression. The boy was not infuriated but tenderly cajoled his father towards a sophisticated behaviour. The man slept later and snored loud, but the boy was alert and the duo got down at Sholapur.

I could now see the mother and the baby at the other end clearly. The baby was beautiful, innocent and most vivid. I could not take my eyes off the child as it was looking at all the passengers with a toothless smile. The baby tried to put its fingers in the food, or tried to pull things. The mother now gently tried to move the baby towards the right behaviour. They put their heads towards each other, laughed and loved each other. I saw that the baby was just six to eight months old but recognized and understood the mother. Not a moment did the mother feel tired or upset with the baby's behaviour. While disembarking I asked her whether I could help her by carrying the baby. The baby though in my arms was watching his mother hesitantly.

These incidents in the train simplified Sheetal Jain's blog on nurturing relations. She says that true relations have to be reared selflessly and tended lovingly as plants to blossom. The young boy was nurturing his relation with his father in the most uncomplaining way and here was a mother who had fruitfully fostered a smile throughout the tedious journey.

I remembered the old couple of ladies who walk together in the evening. One of the old ladies is coaxed every day by her companion towards walking to regain the lost health. She has to use a walker and finds it difficult placing her foot on the path while walking. I was also reminded of the beautiful old married couple who are above seventy years old, who still find themselves lost in each others companionship. The coyness in the lady and the brightness in the man's face portrays the divine life they lead.

Whether it is a relationship between grandparents and grandchildren, a husband and wife, a doctor and a patient, a boss and an employee, a teacher and a student, parents and children or two friends, a bond grows stronger when tended with love and patience leaving no space for misgivings. True relationships have to be reared caringly with faith, warmly with love, genially with togetherness and graciously with patience to help them blossom. True relations need to be tended with adoration and a freshness to keep it going.

"While human nature largely determines how we hear the notes, it is nurture that lets us hear the music."
— Jonah Lehrer

5

AN ACCLAMATION

"The weakest among us has a gift however seemingly trivial, which is peculiar to him and which worthily used will be a gift also to his race" Ruskin

"And you will have to teach 'Insight learning,'" said the Psychology lecturer. He was young and lean, with intelligence written in his amble, talk and conduct. He was one of our favourites, his lectures were one of those few lectures which one yearned to be in, leading to a rejuvenated feel especially after a tiresome lecture of Philosophy. It was an assignment in Psychology for the students pursuing Bachelors in Education at the reputed Comprehensive College of Education in Hyderabad. On reaching home I contemplated on the topic wondering how I would put across the lecture to a class of hundred and above. I loved Psychology as a subject, learning it was easy but to teach the topic required a strategy. I remembered the day my teachers in the senior college arranged a seminar and called us spontaneously to teach. I went confident, but could not teach, I fooled around with the chalk for a long time, looking at my teachers sheepishly, I saw them conversing too, I felt it was most definitely about my helplessness. I asked my friends in the rear about their talk, they said they spoke about the dazzling pendant I had worn around my neck.

I told my father the whole incident exclaiming I would never be able to teach. My father was meticulous, efficient and organized. He rose high in his profession due to these qualities, he was a freelancer and was a part of all India radio for his talks on farming and storage of grains in Telugu, which were scripted through translation of his talks in English.

My father asked me to read the topic deeply, refer books, divide the topic according to its importance and above all plan my lesson. He then told me to go to a secluded spot like our terrace to confer the lecture in an imaginary class. On coming back, he asked me to teach him the same topic, surprisingly I enjoyed teaching him and this time the teaching was far better and more interactive. He raised questions related and I answered with ease. The next day I was all ready for the lecture. I carried a few teaching aids and my father pumped me with oodles of faith and confidence as any other parent.

As I stood in front of the hundred odd students and my Psychology teacher I felt a little shaky, I began slowly in a clear voice and found myself to be at ease, I enjoyed teaching every bit, I carried my smile as my father had told and I found every one listening intently. I used the teaching aids, and involved everyone to interact, and many a time saw my teacher's encouraging looks. At the end of the lesson, my teacher appreciated me and asked the students to clarify their doubts, there were a few questions, but there was one student who stood up and said "I have no doubts for clarification, she has taught it very well". Being young the appreciation gratified me the most.

A new zeal and enthusiasm surged within me towards the profession of teaching. I have thanked my father relentlessly for teaching me the art of scheduling and accomplishing, emphasizing on the ardour God has endowed us with and a never dying faith in God. He was forever there to hearten us whether it was with my research topic or a novelty in the habitual teaching. He believed in the philosophy of "keeping things ready for next use". He wanted us to venture into new forte just as he did and never let life go by without living it the utmost.

Robin Sharma's saying "we are endowed with the capacity for genius. Perhaps you have not taken time to discover what your personal gifts are then honed them to the level where you are considered brilliant" reminds me of the strengths my dad bestowed within me.

This is a tribute to my late father who left us on the 13th of April 2009.

6

THE HOPEFUL

'The signs of success are a smile that does not fade, confidence that does not wither, and a personality that does not get shaken' Sri Sri Ravishankar

The bubbly group of children were laughing and striding ahead. Few of the kids carried a large clean aluminum bowl which was flat on the lower portion as it rested on their head. There was something wrapped in a red piece of cloth kept in the container. I saw the first lot of four children move across the street. It was early in the morning which curbed me from talking to them, but when the second lot was moving across I could not help myself from obstructing them. I peered into their faces. They were all that which any child could be. I could see the smile on their beaming countenance wither as if they were offended. I noticed that the oldest boy was around nine years old and was dressed in a cream shirt and black trousers which were soiled but in an excellent state.

I noticed that the other children who were a few years younger were also well dressed though their clothes were mucky.

They answered my questioning looks saying that they were on the way to beg food. I felt deeply disappointed that the future of India wished to beg rather than earn. They said that they slept on empty stomachs in the night and tried to evoke sympathy while giving me beseeching looks. They did not look like orphans or seem ravenous; in fact they appeared well fed and happy. The eldest one said their parents did not work and so they had to beg. I began searching for my mobile and they crept away. I turned and saw far away the first lot of kids were with a lady who had a half filled white gunny sack. The first lot of children were helping her fill the sack by pouring trash in it. On one hand the mother was making money selling the trash while on the other hand she had transformed her children into vagrants to gratify her immediate needs which she felt were superior to the prospect of making them educated. I realized begging has become one of the easiest ways of making money.

It reminded me of the well dressed lady with a little child inevitably pleading for money. My anger flared as she looked half as old as me and had a vulnerable expression. When I told her I would give her an employment, she walked away never to be found in the vicinity. When I tell young children who are begging for money, to join school and that I could get an admission for them, they sneak away. I had read in the newspapers that the number of beggars in India have increased drastically probably because it is an occupation of earning money with the

21

least effort. The local trains in Mumbai have eunuchs who threaten women in the ladies coach with loud claps, saying that they would place their hand on our heads and all the misfortunes in the world would befall on us. I used to carry a rupee in my closed fist because I was frightened of their looks and behaviour to the core but my friend Nancy would protest and not let me give the money. She was bold and never minded their looks or curses, she would say that we were encouraging begging but I was trying to escape this harsh fact of life by throwing a penny and turning my face away from reality. She cared for the nation and said if all of us denied money to these beggars they would certainly resort to a better form of employment, but for people it is a form of charity to escape from their own sins.

It reminded me of a young lady who lugs a child around six months old while begging in front of a famous sweet shop at Nigdi in Pune. She waves the child's hand to the onlookers converting the child into a beggar before the child even acquires its mother tongue. The irony is that she has begged for years with a child of the same age throughout the year without being in the family way or the child growing. We would always wonder from where she brought these pathetic looking children and we also marvelled at the on goers who never found it strange that this lady got money from them for years together.

At almost every traffic signal we find the old and the young begging with no traffic police to control them. The old require to be empathised and rehabilitated but we found the youngsters and kids smarter in extracting money from people. Many a times when the traffic lights changed to green, the young children would be seen rushing to their mothers to share their booty.

At a church near Kendriya Vidyalaya, IIT Powai in Mumbai, we met a lady who was old and disabled, the watchman of the church told me that she had to factually sleep on the road if no one was able to bring her into the church in the night. I could empathize with the unspoken trauma of this lady. Many of us feel that one life is insufficient to fulfill dreams through the abilities bestowed by God but here we see people of the most striking nation give up their sagacity of strength of mind to just fall back on the left outs of people.

Giving money to these vagrants is a malicious act which may damage their lives by drugs and a misuse of alcohol through overdoses in situations. Perhaps joining an NGO and re establishing people who beg in orphanages with schooling or jobs should be a better option.

"Everyone must leave something behind when he dies . . . Something your hand touched some way so your soul has somewhere to go when you die . . . It doesn't matter what you do, so long as you change something from the way it was before you touched it into something that's like you after you take your hands away." — Ray Bradbury

7

HAIL OR HELL

In bud, or blade, or bloom, may find A meaning suited
to his mind.~Alfred Tennyson

I t was dismal dark, the sky was overcast with clouds,
the intense afternoon's warmth outside had abruptly
cooled, the whole scenario was picturesque and exquisite
with the sky changing its hues, sky blue to deep purple
to grey, there were shades of scarlet and indigo too. The
weary men and women in the huge ground surrounding
the brick kiln had a cheerful countenance as the weather
conditions transformed dramatically into a dreamy one
making the young and the old idyllic. I began stirring in
and out of the porch drawing in mouthful of air while
savouring nature in the startling thunderstorm.

J Krishnamurti in the speaking tree column says 'to
understand beauty, is to have a sense of goodness which
comes when the mind and heart is common.' Who must
not have found the surroundings scenic that day, every

living form seemed elated in anticipation of the unexpected shower. A pair of pigeons were back to their nest earlier than usual to nourish their young ones much before their time. The sky turned darker than ever, and lo behold, it rained hailstones in the month of March. My son who was exhausted after his online exams was quiescent, only to be woken up by his excited mother dragging him out saying 'it never rains hail', and so did all mothers tug their kids who tried to catch the hailstones and gulp it. Within twenty minutes the whole of our lawn area glistened with tiny diamond shaped hailstones, mothers with their little children hurried down the stairs with small steel bowls, they picked the hail and heaped it in the bowl, and clicked photographs to share it with their kith and kin. I sluggishly wandered to get something on film from the third floor to flaunt the beauty of nature while I thanked God to be blessed to witness the appealing environment.

The next day newspapers spoke about the destruction of crops especially oranges, grapes, pomegranates and mangoes. I wondered whether the news was true. Could nature be heavenly for one and dreadful for another?

The joy of the hail storm was so exuberant that the reality was forgotten. Perhaps sorrow is felt only when it thumps the person but joyfulness especially that which concerns nature is felt by all binding us naively in that ecstasy.

A few days back the news heading "Hell Storm" caught my attention. I read it totally as I saw pictures of farmer showing shriveled grapes, uprooted and trampled young banana plants, mounds of half done pomegranates, and a lot regarding the loss each farmer in many of the districts in Maharashtra had experienced. They said the euphoria, exultation and their expectations for a bumper crop fostered for months were ruined in twenty minutes. I remembered that they were the same twenty minutes when we had savoured the hailstones. A farmer said he had to sell the crop of pomegranates for as low as rupees 25000 when he had been hopeful for a fifty lakhs. I felt sad but did nothing.

It was joyful reading today's news which spoke of many of the primary teachers who had decided to donate half a day's salary towards the welfare of the grief stricken farmers. A sum of thirty crores is expected to be generated which will help the farmers overcome their loss. It was wonderful to know that the proficient of nobleness were noble indeed.

J Krishna Murti says that "a shallow mind cannot experience the welling of immense joy upon looking at something when the mind is merely concerned with itself or its own activities it is not beautiful, a mind which is not caught up in its own desires or driven by its own pursuit of success has inward goodness".

Perhaps while enjoying the bountiful nature, each one of us needs to be benevolent in sharing affluence with the unfortunate ones to bring true significance of magnificence in our lives just as the unbiased nature which showers its bounties on the rich and the poor evenly.

'I believe that there is a subtle magnetism in Nature, which, if we unconsciously yield to it, will direct us aright' ~Henry David Thoreau

8

THE BEST THINGS
IN LIFE ARE FREE

"If I had a flower for every time I thought of you...I could walk through my garden forever." — Alfred Tennyson

Nancy was lost in thoughts, her eyes rapt on a boy in the corner of the park. The boy wore an unclean uniform, and was lost in thoughts, seated far away from his friends. It was picnic time, parents had given their kids generous amount of food which they had begun eating right from the time they sat in the bus even before we had begun moving towards our destination. It was beautiful,lovely and an enthralling day, it was picnic time for the students belonging to St'Francis school Vasai. The whole day was blissful with our early morning visit to Essel world in Mumbai. We were the first ones to enter the amusement park. Most of us were teachers in the school, youthful with our students who were merely

seven years younger to us. We were told to reach early
with nothing to carry as teachers would be provided lunch
in the amusement park.

We were delighted to escape the mundane routine.
We loved the amusement park as it said we could leave
our kids as they could move without restraint with their
friends and get into any of the rides any number of times.
The amusement park is one of the biggest ones in India
and a very safe one for children to move freely without
teachers domineering them or expecting obedience
everywhere. We rounded the children counted them,
listed and divided them into groups with a group leader
giving them instructions while leaving them free in the
park as it was out of harm's way. Our team of teachers
broke away into three groups in various directions to meet
for lunch. Essel world was newly built then and indeed
was a huge, picturesque place, we enjoyed every ride with
the kids who would join us. It was lunch time and we were
given a good lunch by the authorities in their restaurant.
My friend looked on at this boy who belonged to std
ninth as he looked at my friend Nancy while she gestured
him about lunch. He told her that he was not hungry but
Nancy cajoled the boy as she placed hundred rupees in
his hand. At Mumbai I always felt children were much
more mature than kids at other places in India. Perhaps
this was because of the fast paced life. They were good
at comprehending a situation or studies in a jiffy. I feel it
must be because of the quality time they spend in schools.
They never have an aversion towards studies as many
of the kids in other cities do due to the long hours in
school. The secondary section closes down by one in the

afternoon as they open for the Primary section, giving time for children to pursue their studies and hobbies, This boy worked in a factory after school to fend for his family. We were young perhaps self-centered in our ways to put aside money for making our stay comfortable but my friend Nancy's gesture puzzled me. Nancy belonged to Mangalore and her husband was working in Saudi Arabia. She never believed in boarding an auto rickshaw in the morning.

I would always reprimand her for saving money by placing herself in discomfort. The auto fare was only rupees two but we had to board a rickshaw from home to station and then station to school and again back. The rickshaws were on sharing basis so we all wished to embark a rickshaw to the school as we boarded the same train. Nancy loved kids and was willing to do anything for them. Many a times I saw her give money to the school children to board an auto rickshaw while she would lovingly ask me to walk along with her saying that I would get a good exercise or that we had plenty of time to reach home with no one looking out for us. It was true as we both were newly married. A few months later I was admitted in the hospital with a miscarriage but Nancy was there every day early in the morning on her way to school with tea in a teapot for me and my husband. I never cried during the trauma but when I met her the bond was so strong that tears gushed out till she consoled me. When she fell sick she never let me know as she lived in on the other side, called the western side, while I lived on the eastern side. One summer I came to know that her mother had a paralytic attack and then she left for Manglore never to return back. We moved away to Hyderabad and things went on but I miss Nancy to this day. She was the first wave of change who taught me that love is greater than money. Money has it own significance but good relations, friends and perhaps a world filled with the essence of life makes it not very imperative.

This life is a gift of love and we love to be loved, to love and to be in love.

9

CAMARADERIE

"Sometimes, reaching out and taking someone's hand is the beginning of a journey." Vera Nazarian

The soft tune of the mobile ring broke the profound silence. My sister answered the phone in a low voice. We could hear her assure the caller that my father was truly at peace then and that he could go to Kerala for his holidays. We understood that it was Prabeesh, the male nurse from Red Cross who had been a help for my father. Memories deluged as we remembered the day he was appointed. He was just in his late teens, lean, bony and shy. He was trained in a few basics of nursing by Red Cross society in Kerala. It was his first job and we wondered whether he could manage my father who was in poor health. His job was to be a companion and look after my father who was gradually losing his muscular coordination due to neuromuscular degeneration. The worst part was my father who could never sit at home, lived a sedentary life. He was intellectually safe. He had slowly begun resigning to his fate. This young boy was trained further and within a few weeks he knew my father extremely well. He would administer insulin injection painlessly; take care of him lovingly in spite of my father's mood swings. He called him 'Muthacha' in Malayalam which means 'Grandfather.' He spoke Malayalam and my father being a native of Alappuzha in Kerala felt at home conversing back. There was a maid to wash and clean, all the meals were provided by my siblings who also got an opportunity to meet them regularly.

Prabeesh was punctual in following the charted timetable while taking care of my father tenderly. As a sport, they played games and playfully he would help my father exercise and practice writing. My father was meticulous, an early riser who wished to have his bath twice a day and all his rituals as he had throughout his life. We felt the adoration and a bond of camaraderie strengthen between them. Prabeesh learnt speaking English and improved on his content through long discussions on various subject matters with my father. They shared their fondness of watching television programs and serials together. He had gained a prominent place in my father's life, and my father would never agree to let him go to Kerala to visit his mother. He once went after three months but returned back soon, the second time he was given a choice of another assignment by the Red Cross who have the work ethics of changing the nurse periodically. Perhaps it was work pressure or an aspiration for more wealth which made him accept another assignment at Hyderabad. My sister in law tried her level best to convince the authorities, but it was vain. My father kept probing about Prabeesh, he missed him, and we could initially see his frustration, slowly the realisation lead him into a depression. He was brave and accepted this reality of life. There was another male nurse appointed from a local hospital, but my father never felt happy with him as he had lost faith in people.

The new Nurse was older and had the least respect for the job. Though we were looking out for a better person we could not get one. One day everyone was ushered at three in the afternoon by the nurse saying that my father was unconscious. It was found that he had left us peacefully in his afternoon nap. I could reach only the next morning. We had begun the funeral rites and it was then that Prabeesh had called my sister from the railway station on the way to Kerala, to enquire about my father. He wanted to come back to take care of my father. My sister felt that she would break the news when he would reach Kerala. We knew the affection he had for my father. Though they were living apart they craved for each other's company, for fulfilling their own emotional needs. Who says indebted bonding is only through blood, bonding is where factual warmth lies. My father's life reminded me of Mother Teresa's words "There are no great acts. There are only small acts done with great love."

A post dedicated to my late father.

10

'Money Money'

Wealth has to be won by deeds of glory. Rig Veda

Money has varied significance and is viewed differently depending upon what it means to the person. It is a retreat for a rich person to spend it while it is a measure to buy basic necessities for a poor person. Money is also viewed as a status symbol as it can buy you diamonds and other possessions to flaunt. People say they are basic necessities, but still money can buy a dwelling but not a home, riches can buy a bed but not a goodnight's sleep, it can buy food but not an appetite or hunger. It can buy a coffin, but not the affection of people who will miss you and mourn for you. These basics are perhaps evoked through goodwill gained by people rather than money earned. True value of money is actually known to those who are in a financial crisis with its need for food and clothing.

Every year an employee is given an increment in the pay. An employed person looks forward to this to plan life with greater purchases like a bigger home and perhaps more comforts, better clothes and accessories. My friend, who is a teacher and who is also my source of inspiration in life informed me about a raise in her pay. She is a Gandhian and believes in the sayings of Buddha and so never feels deeply elated regarding the rise in pay or unduly unhappy in its absence. She also believes in having minimum needs while helping out the poor and the needy. She is a good multi tasker managing her home and job and many other things with great patience never speaking about hardships or her unhappiness. Many a times we do discuss these, but it is always with a positive note that life would have never been wonderful but for these challenges in life which bounce a person back. Off late she had begun taking her mother for an expensive treatment, but still when the increment was announced the first thing she did was support an orphan's meals for the whole year. She told me that our needs are never ending and no amount of wealth can actually satiate the heart of a human being, but a good deed can definitely be a solace.

It reminded me of my student who is in his crucial years of studies. This boy made a place in my heart for having fought difficulties in life with a spirit which no elder can. With a stepmother at home, he did have a number of emotional problems which left him disheartened. He would wash, clean and work at home and still concentrate the most in the class. Over the years, he won over his mother's love through diligence. Money was much-sought after at his home being a huge family with his father being the sole breadwinner. I met him the last time before he left Pune to join his father. I gave him some of my son's books. I asked him to be in touch and to inform me when he needed money. It has been over a year. He has always been in touch to share all his happiness and accomplishments, but has never asked me for any financial help. When I would volunteer he would tell me intensely that he did not need it then.

For the past few months, I was busy in my own world trying to blend in all those wonderful activities of leisure and study that I had, when I left my job last year with my part time job. It gave me a deep sense of understanding that life needs to be enjoyed in tranquility. I have worked for years and have always felt that there was great joy in working and earning money. However, I realized that I never had the time to actually enjoy life as after every Saturday came a Sunday and then it was Monday again. Sundays went in planning and the week went in execution of the plan. Being a school teacher a lot of work was carried home, the small things in life such as a walk, a song, a sketch, a trek and every delight in life including my deep love for nature were far flung. Years flew by and I really wish I had lived these years more joyfully as I do now.

Last week he called me to know how I was. I felt sheepish that I had forgotten this little boy when his endeavors were the greatest being in the twelfth standard. I quickly asked, whether he was fine and did he need anything. The boy paused and said 'teacher, can't I speak to you when I have no problems in life'. I blessed the boy as I enquired more about him, he said that he needed my address with the pin code as he had turned into a tutor and taught a few eleventh standard students. He said he earned a thousand rupees. I was overwhelmed at the gesture. I knew what that money meant for him and his family. He uses his bicycle to commute fourteen kilometer to school, works at home and studies most of his studies on his own never grieving the absence of money or luxuries, but still he felt like sharing his first pay with his teacher. I now realized that generosity and true value of money are perhaps strengths in those who lack it.

> Money is like love; it kills slowly and painfully the one who withholds it, and enlivens the other who turns it on his fellow man. KhalilGibran

11

RESENTMENT AND PACIFICATION

Holding on to anger is like grasping a hot coal with the intent of throwing it at someone else; you are the one who gets burned. – Buddha

The shop owner was a young lady who seemed busy as she handed a beautiful glass framed poster of horses to the buyer. She had cautiously wrapped it with a newspaper and showed the purchaser the way of holding it so that she would not drop it. She was neatly dressed in a saree sporting small pieces of jewellery, her hair loosely tied with a few locks of hair deliberately left to make her look attractive. She was plump and well built. The shop was a tiny one, very near the Mumbai Pune highway, in a lane. The shop had framed pictures of Gods and Goddesses, the sheen of the frames added brilliance to the pictures and the dimly lit shop. The lady was busy attending a Phone call on her mobile, and used crude language while speaking, then her eyes sparkled as she yelled at the speaker asking him to reach early. Just next to her was an inadequate sitting space which was occupied by an old lady. The lady looked old and was wearing a cotton sari with her hair tied in a bun. She seemed tired but still carried an affectionate look which attracted customers.

It was Independence day, the day was drawing to a close with darkness setting in. There were buildings which were well lit. We had got a little time to clean up and catch up with the pending work. Though we had moved into this house more than a year back we never got sufficient time to beautify the house with artifacts. These posters were bought long back, we wanted to frame these.

I asked the lady to show me some sample frames. The old lady handed her a jar, there were a number of samples of frames in it. The young lady tried pulling those rectangular pieces of sample frames but did not get the appropriate one. She turned and yelled at the old lady saying she did not want such nonsense in front of her customers, and that the frames had to be classified. The old lady took the jar to empty the contents on the ground only to be pulled away by the haughty lady as she emptied it on a paper muttering under her breath. I recalled the dragon breathing out fire for now I wished to walk away, but was joined by my husband.

I began to choose the frame as she quoted the rates for framing the posters with glass and acrylic. My husband began admiring the framed posters when his eyes rested on a framed poster of a man. He recalled the person as we had met long back when we had got a huge poster framed. We were surprised to know he was no more. My husband went on recollecting more and more about the shop and the person. The old lady was overwhelmed and had tears in her eyes as she told us that the man died four years back. The young lady looked at her rudely and told us that most of the customers are his old customers. We did not like the resentment she showed in her anger towards the old lady, but placed the order for the posters for the sake of the old lady who lived there after her husband. There was another customer who came in search of a laminated God's picture, but the young lady at the counter had no patience and yelled at her saying there were no low priced framed pictures. I saw customers come only to return back empty handed due to the lady's impatience and short temper. We remembered the owner who was a calm and composed man who loved serving his customers, his customers loved his serene personality and had been his clients over the long years. This young lady seemed to be his daughter in law who was impolite and conceited. Perhaps with time all the old customers who pity the old lady may also stop visiting the shop which was painfully built through love and affection for people.

It reminded me how destructive anger could be. Early in the morning while going to the park, we saw a young pup which was released from its chain, it ran in front of our car. We stopped the car and waited for the man who was ahead to look back, the man in anger hurled the iron chain at the dog which yelped, we wondered whether the reaction was right as the man was boiling with rage early in the morning. Anger causes a rise in adrenalin levels in the blood which increases the heart beat and consequently raises the blood pressure accompanied by a rise in the pitch of our voice, faster breathing rate, tightening of muscles and quiver in the lips with fire-spitting through our eyes which non-verbally conveys nothing but resentment.

Anger can cause strokes, ulcers and diseases while turning into a harsh habit gradually. Anger can be effortlessly conquered, if we discontinue bestowing importance to our ego and practice contemplation, but it is easier when we learn to forgive people and learn to conquer with love.

It is wise to direct your anger towards problems — not people; to focus your energies on answers — not excuses. - William Arthur Ward

12

THE SPIRIT OF LIFE

"The greater part of our happiness or misery depends upon our dispositions, and not upon our circumstances." — Martha Washington

She brought kumkum (vermillion) and turmeric and put a vermillion mark on my forehead with it. She touched my feet seeking blessings and gave sprouts of chickpeas, a coin, flowers, beetle nut leaves and a banana before the gesture. Śrāvaṇa is the fifth month of the Hindu year, beginning late July and ending in the third week of August Shravana(jupaka) is considered to be a holy month in the Hindu calendar due to the many festivals that are celebrated during this time (Wikipedia). She was celebrating Varalakshmi Vratham, a festival followed by the people of Andhra Pradesh in India.

I looked at her as a volley of memories shoved me into my childhood. I could recall Padma aunty standing serenely dressed in yellow and green silk saree with a vermilion mark on her forehead as she yelled and called out our names to collect the Prasad (offerings given to God). She was a good cook and we being Konkani's could never compare our culinary skills to that of aunt's which reflected authentic Rajmundry style of Andhra Pradesh in India. My first memories of aunt are those when I was adolescent. My mother grew closer to her in the absence of my father who was posted at Delhi then. They were constant companions sharing every bit of news. We were perhaps more involved in our lives as youngsters making my mother feel lonely not because of our absence but because of our loss of association of thoughts which she called generation gap. She found great solace in Padma aunty's presence. When I lost my mother, I began noticing aunt more perhaps it was because of the want of my mother. Aunt was a pillar of support to all four of us who had begun life in the death of a mother and the absence of a father who was posted out. At times as siblings, our fights would lead to loud howls, but she was there to take stock of it across our boundary wall. Luckily she got a government job which brought her out of the trauma of losing a friend. Life followed normalcy.

She and I would visit the market to buy groceries and vegetables. Each day I would definitely talk to her across the wall, and I never knew when she had turned into a bosom friend despite our age differences. Her daughter was married and her son away in an engineering college. Her husband was posted at a new place away from Hyderabad. Her job did not permit her to join him. She lived alone not minding the absence as we four youngsters were there just across the wall. Every Shravana she performed this puja called Varalakshmi Vratham, an evocation to goddess Lakshmi. There was gold left in the plate of offerings, but none to walk off with it. I learnt the method of praying from her, but never performed it. We were tenants in the house, and our owner wanted to renovate the house so we moved away into another house a few houses away in the same lane. We found this had depressed aunty leaving her lonely. It was lonesomeness greater than the time she lost her friend, my mother. Though we continued the routine of shopping, the distance had begun distancing our lives. She and uncle would tag me along for the movies they went or to the restaurants they ate at. At home, they wondered at this companionship but I never felt any barriers in communicating to aunty. I would tell her all about college and friends.

On that memorable day I stood outside the gate and called her out aloud, I could only see a bed light through the crack of the window, she never responded to my call. A little later after I returned back buying vegetables I saw my elder sister who was running into one of the houses to make a phone call to the police. Aunty had been out in the market and her house had been ransacked, the lock of her steel almirah had been forcefully opened and all her jewellery burgled. The police dogs tracked the thieves leading the police to a pile of bricks kept in our old house where a short person must have stood on each day to observe her.

Her daughter had been a visitor during the varalakshmi vratam and planned to spend Diwali with her, and so did not feel the need to keep her jewellery back into the locker. I ran to console, as I sat next to aunty, I saw a very strong persona who went through all the formalities courageously. She said the lonely house where we had lived must have attracted these burglars. We asked her to come over for the night as the theft happened at seven in the evening, but she refused and stayed on saying, 'now there is nothing more to be stolen'. She went on with her life and never cribbed about the incident. The police found some of the jewellery after a long time. She bought a whole new lot of jewellery for her daughter and some for herself never giving a thought about the lost wealth. I learnt a lesson of determination and viewing life with what we have rather than what we have lost. Happiness is through contentment which is a condition of mind which arises from the thoughts, beliefs and attitude we support.

"True happiness is to enjoy the present, without anxious dependence upon the future, not to amuse ourselves with either hopes or fears but to rest satisfied with what we have, which is sufficient, for he that is so wants nothing. The greatest blessings of mankind are within us and within our reach. A wise man is content with his lot, whatever it may be, without wishing for what he has not."-Seneca

13

THE COST OF FREEDOM

"The real poetry and beauty in life comes from an intense relationship with reality in all its aspects. Realism is in fact the ideal we must aspire to, the highest point of human rationality." — Robert Greene

The man cycled through the busy streets with a blue drum of water which spilled the water he had painfully procured having stood in a long line. Unhappily he got down to tighten the lid with a plastic sheet to prevent water from spilling. As he began cycling it continued to dribble. The road in the street was burning hot. Each drop of water evaporated the minute it touched the road. There were women who had covered their faces with long pieces of cloth called dupatta in India. The heat was unbearable. Occasionally the sky would turn dark with interspersed heavy clouds giving people the impression that the monsoon would begin but it was a mere illusion. People felt the anguish of heat greater with the reduction in the supply of water. There was hardly any water in the catchments areas, there were very few catchments areas with urbanization and development. Everyone possessed beautiful homes, yet invested in more. The news and media covered the laments of the poor farmers who had lost their crops painfully grown after investing a few thousand to buy crop seeds. The cries of the women whose husbands had committed suicide due to the destruction of crops touched the hearts of people, but they were helpless as the solution was rains. It reminded me of the feudalistic emperors who were cruel yet the people had food to survive. Man is responsible for the passive utilization of nature which has changed with the societal transformation in trade and industry.

Then one fine evening the sky began trickling, a few heavenly drops to be lapped up generously by man, animals and plants. People waited for more, but none came and then it actually began raining. People thanked God for his supreme kindness. The absence of rain had made people understand its value. They bore all the difficulties in going out placidly as they now needed water. It rained every day, each day to the delight of people the intensity grew. We loved it till we heard of the landslide in Pune which had left the whole village submerged with more than hundred and sixty people missing.

The people who were trapped in the landslide were workers who had come to work in the nearby paddy fields. The news said that the ground was saturated with water which caused the mountains tumbledown like a pack of cards. The paddy fields were green with plants but the hutments of their cultivators submerged. People mourned the loss but were no avail. Perhaps it could have been prevented if there were trees planted on the mountains. Their precious lives could have been saved had people not invested in new homes in the nearby areas which used the mountainous soil. The unpleasant incident clearly pictures how a society begins to influence nature.

Unreasonable abuse of nature will leave no resources for human existence. Sensible and judicious uses of natural resources have diminished with the freedom and independence which have led to extravagance and exhaustion of resources in an entrepreneurial system. Are natural calamities in India the price of freedom?

> "In every man there are two minds that work side by side, the one checking the other; thus emotion stands against reason, intellect corrects passion and first impressions act a little, but very little, before quick reflection." — Ford Madox Ford,

14

Trustworthiness

"Most people do not really want freedom, because freedom involves responsibility, and most people are frightened of responsibility." — Sigmund Freud

The young girl ran for a while all along with the bicycle, and as it gained speed she mounted it with ease and crossed through the crowded market. She wore chappals and the road was in a bad state with slush and potholes filled with water which did not deter her. There was a tiny basket fixed to the handle of the bicycle inside which she had arranged a few vegetables, painfully bargained and bought. I kept gazing at her till she disappeared in the array of by lanes at the corner of the main road. It was late in the evening. She must have been fourteen years old but had the mellowness of an adult. As I looked at her, I reminisced the day's happening.

It was a bright morning and the students of the second-year science in the Junior wing were being ushered to the seminar hall. Being new, I could sense they were being led for some unknown reason. Some of the students lingered, we looked on through the doorway of the staff room. All of a sudden we heard a loud yell, the youngster was unmanageable as he burst into tears. We rushed out to find the cause, thinking some mischief was being played. The young boy's friends in reality were trying to console him and told us that the youngster had lost his best friend in a road accident. We tried to console him and made him sit-down. He then told us that his friend was hospitalized yesterday, and had received the news of his friend's death just then. We had to dismiss ourselves to attend our classes. His teacher stayed on.

On reaching home, I read the newspaper to find that there was a head-on collision of a SUV with a water tanker. The news said the SUV(sports utility vehicle) was driven by students who were sixteen and seventeen years old. The news also said that the boys were speeding back from Lonavala in the afternoon. The callousness of the driver of the water tanker had caused the accident. However, the boys who were speeding away had not anticipated the swiftness of the tanker's move. The result was a mangled car and bereavement of the youngsters.

I wondered what made these youthful boys drive a car when the Road transport authorities do not issue a license to youngsters below eighteen years of age. These boys had not reflected the consequences of their action being highly irresponsible. The young girl who was driving away on a rainy day completing a chore for mother was actually displaying a sense of conscientiousness for the happiness of her parents patching her trivial interest for the sake of greater bliss which could have been a beam of a smile on her mother's face. Youngsters never comprehend the trauma their parents would undergo aftermath an accident. Parents spend the prime years of their life in fostering their children not to encash their hardship, but to cherish an objective of contributing their role through their offspring to the world. Perhaps societal transformation can be reassured through a youngster's dependability, but when an unnatural incident snatches their young one due to sheer thoughtlessness an emotional vacuum persists even in the consciousness.

As I read the news I resolved to evolve a new lot of students through my teaching who will value freedom as a task to accomplish greater deeds in life rather than indulge in insignificant actions like driving a vehicle rashly without a thought for the warmth and protection bestowed by their parents, leaving them depart this life in an unlamented death.

> "Character — the willingness to accept responsibility for one's own life — is the source from which self-respect springs." — Joan Didion

15

ALL ABOUT COMMUNICATION

"When the trust account is high, communication is easy, instant, and effective." — Stephen R. Covey

A sugary babyish voice crisped asking, "how much?" making me turn back to have a glimpse of her. She was around nineteen years old, clad in a track suit and a full sleeved 'T' shirt with her curly hair left open. A clump of curls covered her beautiful fair face making her look even more pretty. She had an umbrella and walked uncomfortably in her loose sports sandals. The fruit vendor, a fourteen year old boy said two hundred, now she pointed her finger to the next lot of apples to know the price. He struggled but answered back saying two hundred and sixty. My husband stood at the counter weighing mangoes while I kept selecting a few more. It was bright at about seven in the evening of a weekday. The fruit vendor had the last lot of mangoes called 'Totapari and Kesar.'

This year the market was plentiful with mangoes due to a delayed monsoon. Further, there was a ban on the export of mangoes to Europe on account of a disease in one of the Indian mangoes which led to the assumption that Indian mangoes tend to contract diseases and the European authorities did not want it to spread to Europe.

It was indeed a blessing for Indians who could relish mangoes for a low price. With the arrival of monsoon, the market was flooded with apples but we still yearned for a few more mangoes. The fruit vendor was our favourite as this little boy had excellent traits for marketing. We loved talking to him as he spoke a lot about exotic fruits. He sold both indigenous varieties and exotic varieties of cherries, sweet tamarind, apples, corn, figs and peaches. He would talk about these varieties and try to fascinate us at times. We have always appreciated him because of his integrity and forthrightness and his capability to work hard for hours together. We have seen him begin arranging the fruits early in the morning to packing them late in the night.

During the afternoons, I have seen him recline on a chair but never leave the stall. I would keep asking him to study, he would always nod his head sideways which meant never.

With the girl asking him the rates for the fruits, he struggled to answer his best in English. I now felt the girl might ask him in Hindi, she did utter once 'kitna' (how much) but again stuck to English. We kept watching as the fruit vendor made an attempt to answer in English.

The girl said that she wanted 'four' apples, and began selecting the apples. She was an Indian, but spoke English, her accent gave away and I asked her whether she was a south Indian. She smiled and asked me wondering how I had known it. I smiled back and told her it was her accent which had revealed it. I saw the expressions on her face change as she heard me say that. She retorted immediately saying I don't have an accent. I kept looking at her as she said that she spoke only English and no other language making her more unapproachable. We all were silent on hearing her. I jovially asked the fruit vendor in Hindi as to why he had not learnt English. I saw the girl walk away as the boy kept smiling communicating a lot more through his facial expressions. There is a stress in India on learning English as a foreign language as it is the language of science and technology and a window to the world as proclaimed by Pandit Jawaharlal Nehru, but not knowing an Indian language while residing in India is considered trendy these days and such people are admired for their communication skills. I have heard many say they cannot speak Hindi but are at ease while conversing in English. Any blunder while speaking in English is considered deplorable while that in Hindi is appreciated. Communication is an expertise where the role of language is a mere seven percent, while ninety-three percent includes the non-verbal expression which reveals the moral values of communication. English like any other foreign language can be mastered as a skill with a routine practice but making it a symbol of prestige will unquestionably lower one's stateliness. Our mother tongue is an acquired language, hence gives us a genuineness which perhaps makes one unique while speaking a foreign language. The role here should be to deliver a message clearly, concisely, correctly above all courteously to communicate one's goals and needs to other people.

"You can talk with someone for years, every day, and still, it won't mean as much as what you can have when you sit in front of someone, not saying a word, yet you feel that person with your heart, you feel like you have known the person for forever.... connections are made with the heart, not the tongue." JoyBell C.

16

A TEACHER INDEED

"Teaching is a calling too. And I've always thought
that teachers in their way are holy - angels leading
their flocks out of the darkness." — Jeannette Walls

He had sent me a message seeking my blessings
on the occasion of 'Guru Purnima'. There were
a few missed calls too. Having taken up a part time job
of teaching the undergraduates and graduates in a local
college, I had changed the sound profile to the silent mode.
Guru Purnima is an Indian festival dedicated to spiritual
and academic teachers. This festival was traditionally
celebrated by Hindus and Buddhists to thank their
teachers. It is marked by ritualistic respect to the Guru,
Guru Puja. The word Guru is derived from two words,
'Gu' and 'Ru'. The Sanskrit root "Gu" means darkness
or ignorance. "Ru" denotes the remover of that darkness.
Therefore one who removes darkness of our ignorance
is a Guru. Gurus are believed by many to be the most

necessary part of lives. On this day, disciples offer puja (worship) or pay respect to their Guru (Spiritual Guide). It falls on the day of full moon, Purnima, in the month of Ashadh (June–July) of the Shaka Samvat, Indian national calendar and Hindu calendar. (wikipedia).

I recalled the time when he was a young boy. He was unwavering but he looked out for acknowledgement and an endorsement. I loved all the children in his class as they were from the first day. I was their class teacher for two whole years making me thoroughly familiar with their temperaments. They were naughty, diligent and most helpful, but he rose above others in sincerity. He had an aspiration to learn. Any teaching of mine would be looked upon with zeal and ended with an utmost dedication. I left the school to teach at another school closer to my son's school after a couple of years. The children wept and felt lost, but to this day they have been in touch. They have all done well in life according to their potentials, and have turned into great friends.

He grew along with others, yet he wanted my opinion regarding the college he should opt for while pursuing his studies. He loved his studies, and yearned to carve a niche in the field of education. He had an inborn gene for teaching which within no time turned him into a better teacher than me while managing his higher studies. When we moved to the new home my furniture needed a coat of varnish for a new gleam. The carpenter who had completed the rest of the work was away at his village. He volunteered and got the whole work done by sending a person known. I thanked him profusely as he had saved us from surplus squander of time. He was a self-assured young man now who now had a news of his accomplishment each time we met or spoke. It was never more gratifying for me as I felt I had fulfilled my role in helping a student seek out an identity of his own in achieving his goal.

He was the happiest when he published his research paper. It was even earlier than mine. Now when we discussed, our talks would revolve at the research level. Though our specializations differed, he shared a lot of information which helped me. I wondered how our roles had got interchanged. I looked up to him for learning more and he always had a word of encouragement for me just as I had for him in his childhood. I needed his support for the simple reason that I had decided to continue my studies very late in life. Somewhere I looked at him in awe as he began his studies and teaching students as early as six in the morning. I admired him for that and somewhere felt proud to have taught him, may be it was only for a few years. Today when the call did not materialize, he sent a message seeking my blessings on Guru Purnima. I wanted to know about him as for the past few months I was busy in my own world, he was quick to ask about me and told me that he had qualified his qualifying exam standing second in the college and had got enrolled at the University for higher studies. I knew he had paved his way to success and now needed no acknowledgement while somewhere his inspiration and zeal to progress in life had dispelled the darkness of my apprehensions making him my Guru. On this Guru Purnima I dedicate this writing to him and hope this writing turns into an impetus to all the youngsters in truly fulfilling a Guru's aspiration by being and doing their best to the society.

> "Those who educate children well are more to be honored than they who produce them; for these only gave them life, those the art of living well." — Aristotle

17

CONVICTION

"Have enough courage to trust love one more time and always one more time." — Maya Angelou

I saw tears flow as she tugged my hand and pulled me across, we stood in the line where a mass of devotees stood. We were on the right side, the side where all women stood. It was a special evocation (Aarti) to gain blessings of Shirdi Saibaba, a saint who has been a source of miracle in the lives of his devotees. We stood in deep silence, engrossed in the tranquility and peace of the place. I wondered at the overwhelming response and their tears. Were they tears of joy on realizing truth enforced through trust? They say anguish in one's life spews out as tears due to the undeterred belief in God. The trials and tribulations in life make us powerful and help us grow. My mother would often recite the couplet written by Sant Kabir which summons one to recall God in the good times warding off evils in the bad times while keeping one in bliss thereafter.

I recalled her words when I was upset with the world as I sat in the hospital with my son who was then seven years old. He had got hurt while playing dodge ball. He somehow managed to push his bicycle and come home. I saw his swollen arm, put a sling around his neck after consulting my brother who had suspected a fracture. I took him to the nearby hospital. Tears spilled out of my eyes when I saw my little son in pain. I felt it was great injustice done by God. Now it meant all the treatment and more distress for the child. I remembered my mother's words again and felt God had bestowed us with profuse pain in some way or the other though we were his staunch devotees. We consulted the bone specialist who sent us to the X ray room to know the gravity of the situation. On entering the room I found a young lad left alone on the table. He was an accident victim with multiple fractures. His legs were covered with bandage, his hands and forehead also had bandages. We rushed out in fear. I quickly looked towards the other side to see a lady kneeling down. There was deep grief but she prayed. We went back and sat in the hospital lounge after the doctor treated my son for completing a few more formalities. I saw a young boy speaking to his sister saying that their father should have taken care and also that had their father not climbed the slanting roof this would not have happened. Things began falling in place now. The lady who was kneeling was praying for her husband and these were her children. I began realising that my sorrow was much lesser than many of them around. My son recovered soon and managed fine. We brought him a bigger bicycle and gave enough courage to move ahead. I understood that mishaps are common but we learn to be cautious while taking care of ourself and others by being prudent in life. I realised that God has something in store for everyone, we do get hurt physically and at times a few incidents affect our psyche drawing us into disappointment making one deplore reality, but time teaches us to move ahead in life bringing about the insight that divinity has many more vivid pictures for us to enjoy and rejoice. When this enlightenment draws, tears spill out of our eyes in thankfulness and gratitude for the almighty.

> "None of us knows what might happen even the next minute, yet still we go forward. Because we trust. Because we have Faith." — Paulo Coelho

18

A TRIBUTE TO MRS. NAVALE

"Keep your head high, keep your chin up, and most importantly, keep smiling, because life's a beautiful thing and there's so much to smile about." — Marilyn Monroe

Pradhikaran is a well-planned locale in Pune. Nestled near the post office in one of the lanes in Pradhikaran lived old Mrs Navale. My first encounter with her was when I went in quest of a music teacher to continue learning Hindustani classical Music. She was a retired professor and a teacher who taught Violin to students at their place as a passion. Wednesdays were reserved for vocal music by a sir named Mr. Maltani who came to her place and taught vocal music, harmonium, a percussion instrument called tabla. Harmonium is a type of reed organ that generates sound with foot-pumped bellows. He started at three in the afternoon and taught till seven in the evening. He taught young children, ladies and men. I and a few more ladies and men were taught at 5.30 in the evening. Mr. Maltani taught us classical in the true spirit with a harmonium, an electric tuning box (surpethi) and tabla. Our voices were trained to match the Taal (rhythm) and Laya (melody and tune). Since the classes were just once a week we enjoyed it thoroughly.

Mrs. Navale would also learn vocal singing, but normally her singing would finish before our time. Later she would rush in to prepare a cup for tea for the teacher. Many a times she would be so engrossed in the class that she would forget about tea in the kitchen. Her realization would drag her back to clean up the burnt milk, but she would rush back to the drawing room quickly to resume the class. Mrs Navale was a short lady, slightly on the plumper side with a round face, sparse grey hair on her head which was pulled back into a bun. She wore starched cotton saris and looked very dignified. She was a doctorate and a retired Professor. She used to organize the music classes in the drawing room with the musical instruments which gave a melodious feel. In India, a student sits down with folded feet while singing. The posture gives an easy throw of voice and the lower notes can also be sung with great ease. This posture is considered a mark of respect towards the teacher. Mr. Maltani is a young man with a smiling face and a sincerity which helps any student do his best. Mrs Navale would normally sit on the Diwan with her feet dangling because she could not sit down on the floor.

She would organise teacher's day celebrations for our teacher with great dedication. We would sing our best to please our teacher. On such days, I could hear her vocal singing. She was strong in 'sur' and 'laya' but due to old age her voice many times quivered and cracked.

During the months of July and August the Mondays are considered auspicious being the month of sravan according to the Hindu calendar. She would invite us to give a recital in the temple along with our Sir, Mr. Maltani. We would have steady rehearsals with her cheerful support. During the performance, she would wear her best silks. For a couple of years, I attended the music class regularly but never saw anyone else in her home. I never tried to know about her family. One of those days, I saw her seated on a chair in a gown with her arm fractured. She seemed cheerful and asked us to continue with our class. The young boys and girls and a maid taking care of her had organised the class as usual. The maid kept moving in and out according to her need. A few weeks later Mrs. Navale bounced back into her routine. Life resumed, we participated in our vocal singing wholeheartedly once again. Mrs. Navale would always want me sing Meera Bhajan based on 'Raag Malkose' which had won me a few laurels. The Raag had an alaap which charmed her. I soon got bored of it, but she was never tired of listening. That fateful Wednesday I saw her sitting outside in her veranda with a few more people. She was in a pale cotton saree with no bindi (vermilion mark on the forehead), there was pain written on her face yet she tried to smile faintly. There were four more men and women. They sat away from each other looking at nothingness. She ushered me to go in where Mr. Maltani sat with the harmonium. I looked at him questioningly, he told me in a low noise that Mrs. Navale had lost her husband who was a cancer patient three days back. I wondered if her husband was bedridden, Mr. Maltani said that he had left her for another woman and both the women bore no kids. I felt pained but sang the Meera Bhajan for Mrs. Navale as if my heart would break in grief. Mrs. Navale thanked me for singing the Bhajan.

In the coming months, she was there to guide me to some of the faculty members to seek advice for my higher studies. As luck would have been I got admitted into M.Phil course at IASE Pune. I was managing the course work with my full-time job. Now I found that my interest had begun diminishing with too many things to do. She would always coax me, but I needed to give my time for my son who had reached his tenth standard. When our interest wanes we find many excuses, perhaps it was that which stopped me from continuing the vocal classes. The last time I sang the Meera Bhajan, I was encountered by a hurtful expression on Mrs. Navale's face. I promised her that I would be back in six months. I never had an opportunity to resume my vocal classes as I came to know that Mrs. Navale had a peaceful death on a winter night.

I cross the house many times, I stand looking at the carefully tended sugarcane plants and the huge peepul tree at the gate. I often find myself smiling back at Mrs. Navale's beaming countenance only to be confronted by the forlorn and neglected space.

I feel that God gives a supreme gift to those who are lonesome to befriend people. Mrs. Navale taught me the skill of discovering the inner realm in me with a purpose in life. Her strength to live life in a fruitful way with a determination to move on in life smilingly has taught me a novel way of appreciating and valuing life.

"Why do I take this lonely road, nobody here to walk with me? So I start fresh all over again why won't you just comfort me?" — Sara Quin

19

A GENEROUS CONTRIBUTION

Happiness and a life of deep fulfillment come when you commit yourself, from the core of your soul to spending your greatest human talents on a purpose that makes a difference in others' lives- Robin Sharma

The festive shrieks of the kids made me peep into the open door. I saw a man in pale blue shirt holding a huge blue bag accompanied by a few more people as they called out names. A young girl was given a gift. They asked her to open the gift and show it to the others. The girl could hardly wait to see it. It was a beautiful doll set. I felt it must have been a prize won in a competition conducted. They resumed giving wrapped gifts to each of the children who were present in the gathering. As they got their gifts there were small and loud yells displaying their joyfulness.

I went back and sat in the office. The office at Nachiketa Balgram is a small one with a thatched roof of asbestos in a small clearing paved with shahbad stones. It has a table and a few chairs and a steel cupboard to store documents. Today there were a lot of bananas in plastic bags and a huge steel bucket filled with milk. Perhaps it was tea time for the kids or it must have been a gift by a philanthropist. There were two rooms opposite to the office. One was used as a kitchen and the adjoining room was filled with these kids who were receiving gifts. There was a young girl in salwar kameez with a white dupatta overflowing. She had something in her hand. I asked her what she had received. she brought out a tiny glass box which had a shining wrist watch. Even before I could talk to her, she left the shining watch on the table and went to attend to a chore. She spoke lovingly to a very old lady sitting on the chair in front of the office. I kept looking at the young girl who held all the promises of a beautiful tomorrow with no attachments to material things.

A little later the kids poured out of the room each one having a gift in their hand. There were remote control cars, Barbie sets, books and many different kinds of toys. An elderly gentleman came to enquire about our visit. We quickly told him the reason as he completed the formalities of our visit. Each time we visit Nachiketa Balgram, we have experienced a pure joy in the surroundings. It is not an orphanage which aggravates pity, but is a place which inspires people with the kind of ecstatic bliss. One experiences a deep bonding with the young orphans and the abandoned old orphans. The last time we visited, the whole family at Nachiketa were busy in putting up a programme for the old at the nearby old age home. The loss of parents has given these children a special ability to be compassionate to the young and old.

The students stood in a group and got themselves photographed with the children of a couple who had given them the gifts. Since we were leaving the place together we began conversing. The man introduced himself as Rajneesh, an Indian settled in New Jersey. He initiated a conversation with his wife Monica, his teenage son, daughter and his mother. He said that he wanted his growing kids to know that there were underprivileged kids and that his children needed to know the bliss of sharing a small share of joys with them. Nachiketa Balgram was an endeavour initiated twelve years back with four kids. One of those boys had helped them get a wish list from the children. The man told us that people donate money for the food and clothes, but they never think about the desires and longing these kids have. He said that, they may many a times crave for a new watch or a toy just as any other kid does. He said India would never have been poor, if only the rich could have shared a part of their wealth and their precious time with the needy. I admired the man who gave the little kids memories to cherish through a wonderful evening of conferring joys. Perhaps the poverty in India is actually an attribute of being poor in deeds.

"There is no exercise better for the heart than reaching down and lifting people up" — John Holmes

20

THE ART OF GIVING

"It's not how much we give but how much love we put into giving." — Mother Teresa

He sat on the bench in the garden looking at nothing, his attention focused nowhere. He was dressed in Bermudas and a loose checks shirt which made him appear like a school boy. There was a lady too, in a frock with a walker trying hard to move. The gates were closed but the inner shutters were open. The outer gates were huge with the upper portion made of Iron bars which let a visitor look in. There was stillness which reminded me of fear, death and other ghastly things. I wished I had not come here. Everyone craves to visit a fun filled place booming with joy and laughter,' may be a place where there are new shops or malls inaugurated or where there are carnivals and fairs, a place where people flock. But no one longed to be here. The loneliness was profound with the rustle of leaves, and the groaning sound of a few vehicles passing by. These are the reminiscences of my first visit to this place. A few little kids were sitting outside the gate forgoing their evening play time in all persistence. This was the only spark of life. I wondered where to centre my attention, at the innocent kids or the purpose of my visit. My love won and I began talking to the kids. They all had Plastic carry bags which were empty. They sat silently but spoke to each other in gestures, yet there was a mystery in the air. I asked them in a low sound their purpose. The young kids said they were waiting and gestured their arm towards the guard.

My eyes looked on at the board. It said 'Mother Teresa Home for the Dying and Destitute.' A security guard enquired the reason for our visit. My husband said he wished to meet the head of the home. We were led to the head. My fear overtook me and so I lingered in the garden. My husband went into the neat sparsely furnished office to donate a few clothes and toys. On coming out he said that the clothes would be given in the church as only old people resided there. He also said that the home would like charity useful for the people like toothpaste, soaps, raw rice, lentils etc. This was revealed on my husband's insistence to know what would be useful for the home. I realised that clothes are donated by everyone but money for expenses and the basic needs are mostly overlooked, above all precious time for the needy is never met with. Many a times charity is what we do not fancy at home, in other words we may call it trash. He showed me an open veranda where hot food was being served. The inmates were old and so needed to dine early. They were now slowly pouring out. One of the inmates wandered out till the gate as if he was searching someone. The whole place made me feel weak,here were the destitutes and the dying left by their families. The guard lovingly brought the man back to the seat in the garden and made him sit on a bench. He now looked on listlessly. I wanted to run back home perhaps I was running away from my own conscience. As we reached the gate I saw another person lugging huge vessels of cooked food near the gate. All the little kids were now ushered into the gate where they formed a line and noiselessly filled their carry bags with rice and curry. It was the fresh food left after the inmates dined. The greatest disease is the feeling of unwantedness said Mother Teresa

On one of the visits to the University I was waiting out in the garden. As usual I was trying to sort out and remember if I had finished all that I wanted to do. I saw a young man ushered by his father. The man must have been a student in the university. He had some disability perhaps was a victim of autism. He walked well with his father's support till they reached a place where the path had been dug. Now the boy halted but the father cleverly pulled a leg and placed it on the other side and quickly positioned himself to push him. They crossed the path and the father took him along. While returning back the father took care to change the path to avoid the hitch. I was reminded of the home for the destitute. Here was a parent loving his son unconditionally and there in the home were parents who had been abandoned by their children for having loved them unconditionally.

"Love is not patronizing and charity isn't about pity, it is about love. Charity and love are the same -- with charity you give love, so don't just give money but reach out your hand instead." — Mother Teresa

21

EAT TO LIVE OR LIVE TO EAT

"The food you eat can be either the safest and most powerful form of medicine or the slowest form of poison" — Ann Wigmore

Early Mornings are breathtaking and exquisitely beautiful. We commence our walk around 5.45am when dusk gives way to dawn reminding us that after every gloomy phase there is a striking bright new day, just as a new canvas for a painter to shade life, a new day to set new goals in life, a new day for new accomplishments, a new day for new decisions, a new day to begin life afresh, God lets us understand the intricacies of life through nature. The morning Sun as a red round ball changes the hues of the blue sky slowly gifting all organisms the bodily energy, intelligence and wisdom. Plants gain their source of energy from the sun and share it with all other living beings through the creation of food. Food is an imperative need in our life.

I saw a few middle aged men rush back after their walk cheerfully. Durga Tekdi is a picturesque hilly artificial forest with a laid walking area at Nigdi in Pune.There are a lot of vendors outside the gate who space themselves to sell fruits and vegetables on the long roadside selling farm produce using the word in vogue 'Organic.' There is a young boy who sells fresh fruit and vegetable juice for the early morning walkers. He makes his little venture attractive by placing the steel containers containing juices on a table, lights incense sticks to give a special aroma to his place, a few glass bottles containing ladoos made of groundnuts, sesame etc are placed to attract kids and adults.

I saw those young men rush to have their daily health drink, but their hands led them to pop a few of the ladoos quickly to satiate their craving for food. It was just six thirty in the morning making me wonder 'how hungry can man get in a three km walk.' They now rushed to the fruit stall and bought a few fruits. As they were buying they planned to make a fruit chat out of it. The first few hours helps us organise our day well when we are able to retain silence. Internal quietness is mastered through a routine practice like meditation which helps to develop a sereneness and poise within. This also helps us to overcome cravings and teaches restraint.

People say we need to 'eat to live' but with technological development the perception has changed to 'live to eat.' Technological progress has led to a change in the standards of living for everyone. We find people shop in malls and bazaars. They enter with a trolley to shop, and the mall owners lay bait for the customers offering attractive offers on food items. Many a times the customer does not require the quantity but buys it to save a few rupees not realizing that they have created a demand for the item in the market leading to a rise in the price of that product. After shopping, the food has to be cooked and eaten before the expiry date. There is greater quantity of food cooked. This leads to obesity or latent obesity. These food items are not safe if they are processed food. Perhaps an obsessive compulsive disorder has set into the pattern of eating as people eat anytime and any quantity of food they come across. Weddings, parties or get-togethers are lavish affairs with food served beyond the capacity of eating. People eat more than required when it is freely available.

We had a meeting on the Independence day many years back in one of the school's I worked for. The aroma of Vada and sambar combined with Gulab Jamun an Indian sweet threw me into a bout of hunger I had never felt. My friend a Gandhian refused to eat. On coaxing her she just asked me 'is your stomach a dustbin where you keep dumping food any time,' it is an organ which needs to be respected like the brain to function better, perhaps it was her thought which changed my world. It was difficult to develop a moderation but now I am able to master it as a habit. It helps to eat quality food at the right time.

It reminded me of my childhood when sweets and savories were only a part of festivals. I remember my mother and our neighbours call a few young ladies to help them in pounding rice, Dal and chillies to make these savories with the special interest and pain to make them healthy.It taught us restraint and an ability to enjoy the festival utmost by making it special. Money has taught people to buy 'ready to eat' foods and sweets any time leading to flabbiness. The batter of Idlis and Dosas are also bought to save time. Every week people specially eat out to take a break from home made food stuff which bores the younger generation who loves Pizzas, hotdogs, chocolates and aerated drinks. The younger generation also gets sufficient pocket money relieving their parents from packing homemade lunch to eat their choice of pastries, scones and burgers. They have grown lethargic and obese with a constant craving for food. Their sluggish walk and their behaviour depicts that they no longer have the self-control to choose the right food. Eating foods which have excess of fats and sugars reduces the inspiration and sets in lethargy which sucks away the energising stimulation and the will to be agile. Eating healthy food in the right quantity at the right time keeps one in the pink of health formulating the saying 'eat to live' come true.

"Eating healthy nutritious food is the simple and right solution to get rid of excess body weight effortlessly and become slim and healthy forever" — Subodh Gupta

22

APPARENT ADORATION

"Every parent is an artist, but not every artist is apparent" — Eric Micha'el Leventhal

It was late evening, in fact, it was almost dinner time, but the little girl wished to play. I saw the mother pondering for a while, maybe she hoped to prioritize the needs of the child. She sighed, but let the child have her way. I saw them run all over the place, shrieking and enjoying every bit as they kicked and shuttled the ball on the lawn. I watched the little girl fall several times, but so great was her enthusiasm that she stood upright within a second. After a while, I saw a contented mother and her happy little daughter climb up the stairs wearily to go home. The mother had forsaken her timely duties and awarded beautiful moments for her daughter to cherish.

Memories deluged as I remembered the growing years of my son. After school in his kindergarten, we would never return back home without playing in the play area of the building for a long time. He taught me batting, bowling, dribbling and made me a complete person by evincing my interests in boyish sports. When he was five years old, a programme of integrating teaching with the use computer technology was launched by Intel to make teachers technologically savvy. I was attending a few extra courses at the Don BoscoSchool, Hyderabad in summer. Since the school was just a few km away from our home, I would walk and my son would accompany me on his bicycle. He would sit and watch me learn, perhaps the deep interest in computer engineering might have been due to this precursor course.

Now at nineteen he is my best teacher who not only helps me with the technology but shares all my interests of music and art. When he began playing guitar at the age of ten, I began learning Hindustani Classical. We were an excellent team in merging classical notes with western. The whole journey is a memorable one making me thank God incessantly. My husband's transfer to Konkan brought me and my son closer. I feel children are true mirrored reflections of their parents. A poise and composure in me was bestowed with the growing years watching the goodness and innocence in my son who has learned to respect people for what they are rather than what they look like or have. My greatest lessons in life were learnt with him as a friend. We do trouble each other, but I learnt that a change in ourselves is a must, if we wish to see the change in our child.

Robin Sharma says putting one's family at the top priority along with one's health is utmost important.

Time flies and so do children grow. Many of the parents stay away from their families for earning a better livelihood and providing the best to their kids. The child deprived of the parental love loses the affection of the parent in the formative years and grows arrogant with the money gained from the parent to overcome the guilt of neglecting the child. When a child lives with his parents, seeing them struggle for a living teaches him the best lessons in life. The mellowness gained while helping one's parents makes them responsible in life.

A fear created in childhood by parents, teachers or friends become a hurdle in the mindset of a child. We find children hesitantly looking at their parents before taking an initiative because of the fears the parent has associated the child with. Children grow well when they watch their parents as examples of inspiration. Many of the parents want their children to study while they indulge in idealistic talk or watch television. I have seen my friends and many parents turn into role models for their children by perfecting their lives while many more ruining the lives of their children through neglect and overindulgence.

Perhaps parenting is an art like listening. A barrier in the approach of the parent is an obstruction in the frame of mind in the child. Trust, amnesty, accountability or adaptability are gifts subtly conferred to children through quality parenting.

Ruskin Bond values the parental relations above all pressures and impulses in life. His childhood wistfulness of unhappy days persists in his realization signifying the disturbing emptiness. Bond feels that parents are responsible for their children and should mend their differences as the child has an undeniable right upon his parents love logically.

> The love a parent has for a child, there's nothing else like it. No other love so consuming." — Cassandra Clare, City of Ashes

23

THE MERCIFUL

"He who has a why to live for can bear almost any how." — Friedrich Nietzsche

The street was overflowing with people, it seemed very narrowly laid in the vast spread of greenery. It was vacation time for the kids in North India, in South India the schools reopen in the first week of June. People love being at Shimla in Himachal Pradesh in summers, it was the summer capital during the British rule, it has a pleasant weather being a hill station. There were people of all age groups. Every one seemed affluent and well-groomed as they made their way towards an opening sporting two lifts. One has to pay rupees ten to go to mall road in Shimla via this lift. The lift carries eight people at a time, moves half way up and then we need to walk through a by lane to enter another lift which carries us above the hills on a steep mountain road called the mall road which has several small shops lined on either ends.

There are a few diversions which lead us to clearings where there was a church, temple and a summer festival was also going on in a large clearing. It turned warm with the rising sun and speeding up crowd, shopkeepers began briskly selling their wares, we trudged on searching for something special for our kith and kin. After the shopping we looked around for the lift area, but it seemed very far, however we saw a narrow staircase moving down to the area where our car was parked, we moved down regretting our decision as the stairs were narrow and uncomfortably crooked that made the descent very difficult. I looked around to see a person fair and strongly built, who was gradually moving along the mountain slope towards these stairs heading to mall road. The only distinction was that he was hauling a brand new refrigerator in a brown carton strapped to his back. There was total indifference to this sight which made me understand that it was a common spectacle, a little ahead I saw men and women awaiting to carry sacks of onions to mall road high up on the road, mind you the sacks were a hundred kilos and above. On questioning I came to know that these scenic tourist spots had no source of employment for the localites, and as they heaved weights they reminded you of animals used for dragging loads reminding me of ancient Sumerian world, when human beings were used as beasts of burden.

At the hotel I met stewards who were working as room service boys and errand boys in spite of a degree in Hotel management for rupees 4500 per month. They lived in pathetic condition in the villages in small hutment resembling the slum areas in Mumbai.

The women who lived in villages walked the steep mountain roads covering long distances to sell wild berries and cherries. They pleaded people to buy it but people prefer buying cherries which are presented well in beautiful packed cartons as it looks hygienic, fresh and is easy to carry along. The most common means of travel in these places were tourist cars, but the tourist loved mounting horses and yaks and took numerous pictures to post it on social sites.

At Kufre, 20 km away from Shimla, I noticed many horses and a few yaks. The localites use these as a means of transport on the steep mountains. They either use these animals or just slide through the short cuts formed due to soil erosions in the mountain valley where there are monkeys, bears snakes and other animals to reach their homes in the valley. Many of the localites moaned of having been bitten by snakes, and then were brought back to life when one amongst them would suck the poison out. They had never heard of antivenin and I did not know an equivalent in 'Himachali' a language spoken in Himachal Pradesh. These localites had a perfect indulgence with the car drivers, who were arranged by make my trip, yatra. com or any other tourism department to take tourist for a horse ride with a directive to pay some amount to the driver.

We often found the innocent localites earning lesser than the cab drivers who were shrewd being city bred. We had a young boy who took us to the snow point, high up in the snow clad mountains. We were asked to hire clothes, gum boots woollen socks by warning us that we would freeze on the Himalayas, we found everyone akin, and so paid three thousand for those few hours. The lad promised us Ice skiing on the iced slopes of the Himalayas.

During our interaction we understood that the lad hardly got any money in the transaction and his whole day was spent in being an itinerant. Further, he said that the tourist jobs were only during the tourist seasons in summers and in winters. During the rains they needed to look out for other jobs. We however found they were the most loving people despite their hardships. They had a great deal of decency, goodness and dependability which by no means is found in developed states. They were kind, sympathetic and spent all their valuable time while we kept aping at their vulnerability and inability to get a proper job. They were worse than those daily wage labourers who at least have a job, these men need to look out for a different job each day according to the season.

It reminded me Jug suraiya's article 'what a waste' in Times of India where he says that financial desperation inspires Indians to move to alien lands despite the fact that they have to learn new skills, keep out of the punishments and law, learn new language and try to survive in the hope of earning wealth in a distant inhospitable clime. They may not cause a brain drain like professionals however they are no less witty with strong innate abilities which have helped them survive.

Conceivably a country grows when the people are able to endure and contribute in their own capacities. Himachal with its unstinted environment should have been a challenge for any other state in employment and wellbeing of its people.

"We are products of our past, but we don't have to be prisoners of it." — Rick Warren

24

HASTE MAKES WASTE

"Patience is power. Patience is not an absence of action; rather it is "timing" it waits on the right time to act, for the right principles and in the right way."
— Fulton J. Sheen

People have a weird way of reacting in situations. Some ignore and walk away displaying inhumane feelings while the others enjoy helping out and spend their whole time in that situation, living it every moment. If a person falls down or collides with a bus or any other vehicle within minutes you will find a crowd of people in India. They leave their vehicles aside. Pick the person, dust him, calm his agitated nerves, pick his vehicle and leave it aside. They may enquire the person's wellbeing then and wait till the hurt person goes back. If there is a problem like a fire or shortage of water or a quarrel, we find these people running about and not resting till the situation is under control. These are looked upon as volunteers and are highly respected in India. Perhaps it is their interest or may be the desire to keep busy when they have nothing to do, which motivates them.

The floods in Jammu Kashmir were taking toll of people reminding me of the gravity through a day's experience during one of the monsoons in Pune. The rivers were overflowing. It was a bountiful year with plentiful rains. The dams had released thousands of cusecs of water and the city was submerged to a small extent. The newspapers carried the pictures of the submerged Mourya Goswami temple at Chinchwad with only its shrine visible. We still were living uphills and were lucky. That afternoon there was water left in Indrayani river near Dehu Road and so great was the water level that the water rushed downstream to Nigdi and filled all the low lying areas on the Mumbai Pune Highway.

My son was a little boy who was eight years old then. He was studying at one of the Kendriya Vidyalaya which did not have a bus facility for the students. He used to travel by a van with other students. That fateful afternoon he did not return by the usual 2.30 pm making me visualise a misfortune. The weather had changed. It was sunny, but the roads still had water which did not seem to recede. My husband was posted at a remote place in Konkan making me all the more responsible for my little boy. I drove my scooter precariously through one small stream and reached the crossroads where water was flowing seemingly fast. I saw a group of people guiding others as they crossed on their bikes. Some were wading in the water to reach their destination. My goal was just twenty meters away which could lead me to the school from there. As I began driving, the group waved their hands while standing in water asking me to go back. I felt pity surging within me for me and my son as two lonely beings, and decided to move ahead. As I drove in the water I grew dizzy and felt strange as if a whirlpool was gripping me and then I fell, and slid with water.

My scooter was nowhere; I was picked by people who yelled saying that they had cautioned me. I felt embarrassed but quickly said 'my son'. Some more people at the other end caught my scooter and brought it out. But one group started rushing downwards as if they were searching something. A few dangerously bent in water to pick things. Someone then asked me where my son was. I said I was searching for him. Now they rushed a little downwards and said that they needed to prevent the baby from going down the open drain. One of them asked me how old was my son making me realize that they were actually searching for my son. I told them in Hindi that I had come in search of him and that he was eight years old. I quietly pulled my scooter and came out of water helped by a few people. But for these volunteers, I would have landed down the open drains. I was hurt as I had landed on the rocky surface of the road underneath the water. On coming out, I found my arms and feet smarting and bleeding. I felt I would go back home and decide what should be done. Sadly I drove back pitying my situation. On reaching home I found my son playing in the garden, he came rushing to hug me. I prayed God a prayer of thankfulness for bestowing my little one safely back to me. I thanked those volunteers who were socially responsible from the depth of my heart for having saved me before things got worst. It taught me a lesson of patience and wait before rushing to conclusions however emotionally bound we are. Patience gives the power of endurance in dire circumstances and presents a serenity to do things right while impatience evokes annoyance. Many a times a person takes hasty and impulsive actions to repent in solitude.

"It is very strange that the years teach us patience - that the shorter our time, the greater our capacity for waiting" — Elizabeth Taylor

25

A NOVEL FRIENDSHIP

Ruskin Bond feels being alone is accepted as an individual seeks it, while loneliness is the curse of being alone without a companion when a person yearns for a friend.

Mega vision diagnostic scan and X-ray centre is a popular one located a little away from a Mosque near Nigdi Bus Stop in Pune. It is accessible through Pradhikaran too. My annual sonograph to check multiple fibrosis was due for long. A faculty meet and development programme in the afternoon gave me some free time in the morning. I took a quick decision and raced through the by lanes on my scooter to reach the place. The intention was to be the first and return back soon. In my enthusiasm, I had raced a little ahead of the place. I tried turning back with a little effort as the road was inclined. It was eight in the morning, but the whole locality was quiet. There was a voice from nowhere saying 'it opens at nine'. I turned to glance at the person. She slowly walked towards me with a file and a bag and said that she was also waiting for the centre to open. She seemed middle aged and was draped in a saree and carried a grave expression on her face, yet there was a charm which attracted me towards her. We waited for a while in one of the rooms. There was a maid who was cleaning. A little later as people began gathering, we went towards the gate leading towards the scan and X- ray centre. By now the lady was almost a good friend. She had come for a X-ray of her backbone. She explained her entire journey of pain leading to a kind of spondilitis. She then asked me about my problem. I was in two minds whether to begin my expedition of problems or just tell her that it was a regular sonography, but before I could speak I saw a radiologist come in. We waited for some more time for the gates to open. We then went into a clearing adjoining the X-ray department and a sonography room. Many people can get their scan taken at an instant because of many cubicles with sonography machines installed.

We paid the fees and sat there in the lounge. She now quickly pulled out a smart phone and showed me her daughter's dance photographs, and then showed me the photographs of her son who she said was just eight years old. She said that she was a little above forty years old but seemed worried about her health. I just gave her an empathetic listening. I learnt that even this helps people overcome their pain. She asked me doubtfully 'you must be having grown up children', I nodded and approved. She kept saying 'what if the result says that there is a swelling in my vertebral column', I smiled and said, 'everything must be alright, please don't worry and be positive'. She said that off late with the disease gnawing her, she was terribly worried. She said she wanted her husband to accompany, but he had left her and gone back home. She looked at me, I said my husband was managing the home as the maid comes early. She asked me whether I was not frightened. I was praying God that everything should be normal, but felt she needed greater assurance then. I smiled and said that we enjoy what we have today rather than think about what is going to happen. She quickly took my telephone number and said that she was an entrepreneur who managed a shop at Pimpri.

By now she seemed a little more confident. She told me that as soon as we finish our tests we will have the coffee she was carrying in a flask. The lady at the counter called her, she left her bag with a nod. The sonography machinery was still being started, the Doctors moved idly while I kept praying God to help me get through. She came out after fifteen minutes. The sonography machines were still not ready. People were drinking water with a retaliation as a scan needs that. She smiled and heaved a sigh saying its over. I was called in and luckily as the doctor read out the measurements I heaved a sigh of relief. It seemed ok.

On coming out I rushed to go, she was still waiting but rushed out along with me. She said her husband would come, but she would get her report in another fifteen minutes. She caught hold of my hand and looked deep in my eyes with an approving thanks and asked me to drink coffee. I knew she needed a companion, but it was late and I had to rush back to home. She pulled me to a small Saibaba temple at the cross roads saying 'let us pray Baba, he does wonders'. I stood there with her. Faith moves people while building up courage. I waved her and started my scooter, only to find a hand resting on my arm saying, 'do not drive hastily, take care'. As I drove I wondered how people bond with each other in adversities. It compelled me understand that those few minutes of difficulty needed assurance that we still had life to look forward to. Perhaps it was mere strengthening of bonds of love and affection between two lonely people by being there for each other without hurting sentiments reminding me

"None of us knows what might happen even the next minute, yet still we go forward. Because we trust. Because we have Faith." — Paulo Coelho, Brida

26

Positive Reception through words

"It's funny how, in this journey of life, even though we may begin at different times and places, our paths cross with others so that we may share our love, compassion, observations, and hope. This is a design of God that I appreciate and cherish." — Steve Maraboli

The speaking tree column by Janina Gomes 'Know That You Have it in You' on the 28th Feb on contempt left me contemplating the vast and diminutive issues which may have influenced one's life in their personal sphere, at their workplace or in their social life. It said contempt for anybody- the less privileged, the vulnerable people of other faiths, women, those who live independently, the differently abled -the mentally challenged could percolate down the different strata of society. It set me pondering on the saying as it definitely confirmed how people enjoy hurting others and inflicting pain through words of scorn and hatred. It reminded me notably of the incident which occurred a few days back.

With the onset of spring the days have slowly begun turning hotter. It was one of these hot afternoons when one could feel the high temperature in the atmosphere. The play school children who normally linger in the garden with their mothers till half past one had gone back home. The watch man was back into his cabin after his rounds and the stillness in the building complex and on the roads was significant. I heard the loud resonance of our calling bell and rushed to the door hoping the visitor wouldn't press the bell a second time due to the impatience I felt in the first call. I peeped through the peep hole to see the figure of a woman with two long sticks very close to the grill door, stopping me from opening the door. I now peeped cautiously and found that it was none other than my maid. I quickly opened the door wondering what had gone wrong as she had finished her work in the morning. She had bought two long cobweb brooms and stood in the corridor for approval. She looked worn out with the day's work, the chill in the early morning and the afternoon heat had left her skin dark dry and shrunken but still, she looked at me hopefully for a consent. I looked at her inquisitively as she beamed and reminded me that I was the one who requested her to bring it. I acknowledged nodding my head and asked her the price so that I could pay and send her off but she wanted me to know that she had found the vendor faraway when she was returning home and had come to give it as the vendor would not be allowed in the premises. Perhaps my curtness for paying the money made her sad as I could sense her disappointment. I hastily smiled as I asked her to give the cobweb broom. She asked me my choice and tore the plastic sheet from the covered head to show that she was giving me the better piece and it was actually a better one with a static broom head while she kept the plastic broom head for herself. I rushed in and brought a hundred rupee note and thrust it in her palms. She looked at me saddened and said that she had paid the hawker and did not need the money immediately. I told her that I could forget the transaction and compelled her to take it and sent her home so that I could continue the incomplete work which was left. I understood that she wanted to be approved for having been practical

The next day when my maid came for work I told my husband that she had bought the cobweb broom relinquishing her precious time in the afternoon.. This was to help my maid over come the disappointment she had felt the previous day. She was pleased with the appreciation and explained the whole deal to my husband in Marathi with a quiver and a shrill pitch in her voice which justified the delight she felt. Janina's column reminded me that how contempt surges with ease for the under privileged. My maid had trusted me with her money but would I have the same faith first if I had mislaid anything at home? The burglary in one of the flats had evidences pointed at the maid first and then at the watchman. We not only hold them responsible but shower words of disapproval rather than appreciation. Janina says that those who hold others in contempt do so out of their own inadequacies and frustration and that those who know the true meaning and purpose of life uplift lives through appreciation. It also helped me figure out how a optimistic person finds the world positive and the words delivered by such an individual are never mocking or sarcastic while a person filled with resentment tries to haul words of hatred, conceivably trying to experience peace for himself in the deliverance that life has been harsh towards him. The elation felt by my maid for having been useful to me was great strength and joy for her as reflected in Janina's words which say 'Appreciation heals divisions,builds bridges and adds to our strengths,it helps us with self affirmation and brings positive forces into play giving the 'Feel good' Feeling.

Lets resolve to stop being unkind and traumatise others with words of contempt and make the world a better place to live.

"Appreciation is a wonderful thing. It makes what is excellent in others belong to us as well." — Voltaire

27

THE IMPERFECTION

The marketplace was crammed with wares. New shinning steel utensils, latest cookware, gas stoves, dish stands and many more festooned the steel shops. The flower vendor had an unusual order of sacks of marigold flowers; there were pale yellow marigold with smaller florets and finer petals. The orange ones were the poor man' delight which was low priced. The shop keepers had a tough time overseeing the sales and the orderliness of their shops. The shops had to be cleaned and the pictures of Gods also needed the obligatory gleam after all it was to summon the goddess of wealth. Yes, it was all groundwork for the laxmi pooja, the goddess of wealth and prosperity. Few were getting their houses painted, yet others were emptying the junk away from their homes. Every one seemed busy and eventful abruptly with an evocative seriousness which a marathon runner faces when he stands ready to out beat all to prove a do or die situation. Aroma of goodies was wafting out of kitchens. Chakli, chudha, ladoo and many more savouries were cooked choice fully. Away from the buildings in the shacks and shanties tired mothers were returning back home. Their little children came, running and tearing the streets to reach them. There were girls and boys who could be no more than five to six years of age. Two babies were being lugged by their elder sisters. It was Diwali, the festival of lights, fervour and delicacies. They felt the pangs of hunger as they saw their mothers. Their mothers were not maids working in the houses of rich men who would give away stale food on the name of charity to cleanse their sins. They were the daily wage labourers who were over exerted with the on coming festival. Mothers hushed the children and cajoled them to play for a while more while they started their kerosene pump stoves in haste to cook for their little children.

The children gaped into the park of the new residency where their role models, the affluent kids wearing expensive clothes carrying playthings and crackers dawdled around. They forgot their hunger for a while and gazed at them. They vied these kids for their prosperous life. They wanted to be akin to those rich kids whom they had been watching for days together. After a while when the kids stopped playing, the gang of kids from the shanties ran to the place where the rich kids had burnt crackers, they stooped down and picked the partially burnt crackers, dusted it and pocketed it. They tried to walk like them in the used slippers thrown by those rich children. Still later after a dinner of sparsely cooked vegetables and rice, these underprivileged kids had a game of mimicking the rich children when they tried wearing the clothes given away in charity and the boys toyed rolling a round pipe on PVC pipes making it their future rolls Royce. The irony was they impersonated the hypocrisy, the pretence very easily just as the rich who mimic their sincerity in the name of God dreading that the wealth earned might be lost in the wrath of the Goddess of Wealth. Wish they could mimic the uprightness and respectability of simplicity and humility instead of the façade. Wish the rich kids could role model the significance of education for these children rather than deceit. The imperfection lies with the pretentious elders who have marketed falsehood.

A post dedicated to my friends Vimala and Durga who have initiated their first step in societal transformation.

28

A CARING HEART

The wedding preparations were in full swing. Kaaki was cheerful and perpetually had a beaming smile on her face. She was a proud mother with her two fair,tall,fine-looking sons who were well settled. Her would be daughter in law belonged to a wealthy family at Mahim in Mumbai where most of the affluent Gujaratis resided. It was prestigious when a family owned an accommodation in central Mumbai or near about for those Urbanites who reside in western suburbs. Mrs Patel was addressed Kaaki despite the fact that she wasn't many years older than us as she got married at the age of eighteen and was blessed with two sons before her twentieth birthday and her life revolved around her family. She entered the family as a young bride to take care of her husband and father in law as this was an elucidation provided by nature when the lady of the house was no more. Kaaki treasured serving people and executed her house hold chores with utmost sincerity. Her evenings were spent meeting in the open expanse of the flat were most of the ladies gathered. The younger ladies lingered for their husbands and the older ones hung on for their sons and daughters. There were many who would bring their little children to amuse themselves. Kaaki always had a recipe to share or a household remedy for a common ailment which every one of us loved to know. Her elder son Madhav was employed in a multinational and his fiancee was a petite attractive girl working as a fashion designer. I remember the time he brought the pretty girl home when she was a cynosure of every one's eyes.The wedding was fixed after Diwali during the auspicious wedding period. One of the reasons for arranging the wedding early at an young age was that, of late Madhav's grandpa was not keeping well. Just a week before the wedding he developed a stomach infection and had to be hospitalized. He recovered enthusiastically within three days and was brought back home. Now there was nothing to dissuade the spirit. There was a ritual of smearing turmeric paste on the boy and and tying an amulet so that the on coming rituals were not impeded in any unforeseen circumstances. Relatives had assembled and there was fun and frolic. Mothers were eventful in arranging things for the rituals and ceremonies while fathers and cousins had gathered down and had begun bursting crackers. First it was string of bombs and then they got into the doldrums. There were flower pots burnt but each one waited for their turn to burst a laxmi bomb or a hydrogen bomb. In the stillness of the night we could perceive loud sounds for a protracted time. Every one of us was disturbed but didn't have the inclination to communicate our exasperation.

At around 11.30 pm there was silence and we all went to slumber only to be woken by loud howls and laments. The heart rendering cries dragged everyone to Madhav's home. His grand father was still and lifeless. He was quickly taken to the hospital only to be declared dead due to a massive heart attack. The last rites were performed the same night. As the wedding couldn't be deterred, Madhav left for his marriage with his brother and got married. It was deplorable. I was reminded of this happening because of the callousness of the young who derive pleasure in loud boomeranging sounds accompanied by clouds of smoke which are harmful to the asthmatic, the old and ailing. Lets foster empathy, an indomitable spirit and a deep concern to conquer desires which confer pleasure for self but destroys others peace, harmony above all subsistence of life.

29

A REFLECTION OF THE CONTEMPORARY WORLD

I know of no more encouraging fact than the unquestionable ability of man to elevate his life by conscious endeavour -Henry David Thoreau

It was late in the evening. Me and my husband were rushing back home after a customary visit to the kocchu Guruvayur temple at Nigdi which is a miniature Guruvayur temple at Trissur in Kerala. We had parked our car in the by lanes of Pradhikaran which is a well planned locale at Nigdi and walked to the Temple. In reality we find these walks irresistible as we are able to meet people and we rejoice looking at the far off starry skies, the exquisitely lit monuments and the demanding market. Nigdi is known for Bhakti Shakti square where Emperor Shivaji's and Saint Tukaram's huge statues have been mounted at a height depicting Shivaji's undying faith in his teacher. It is surrounded by green vegetation and curved paths leading to the figurine. As we entered the open area we met Mrs.Varghese who has been a good friend of ours for the past eleven years. Our friendship dates back to the year 2002 when we had begun living at Siddhivinayak Nagar connected to Durga Tekdi, a man made forest on a terrain of more than 3 km expanse. The forest is normally used by people for morning walks. There are many courses to reach the summit. People change their routes according to the time they are able to spare. I met Mrs.Varghese for the first time at this place when I was introduced to her through a mutual friend. Mrs Varghese lives in Pradhikaran in an apartment close to the road leading to Appughar and Durga Tekdi. A few years ago she had lost a chain with a pendant when some chain snatchers had assaulted her at the crack of dawn during her walk. One of them had gagged her to muffle her voice and the others snatched her chain. Later they had jumped off into the adjoining area called transport Nagari which is a depot to park huge transport vehicles. After the incident Mrs. Varghese had stopped coming for walks in the wee hours and wouldn't sport a chain. She was aggrieved by the offenders who were juvenile like her own son. She had worked as a teacher for a long time and of late had resorted to educating a few kids taking private tuitions at home. As she noticed us she smiled affectionately and told us that she had been praying God for a companion to walk back home. We treaded along with her as we could converse a little longer. The picturesque long lane from Hotel Vrindavan at Bhakti Shakti to her home was nearly a ten minute walk. She was clutching a few things. We shared the load and began enjoying the stroll and the chatter. As we crossed the beautiful huge mansions in the dimly lit street, she stated that the place had become notoriously insecure. She had lost another chain and lately while she was returning home from a friend's house at eight in the evening, two adolescent boys had grabbed her handbag containing money and all indispensable documents. She felt hurt at the loss but more than that she was distressed at the attitude of those young boys who had learnt to acquire riches through the impairment of the physically weak. She said that she felt awful having lost the hard earned money. It pained us all the more as we both have sons round about the same age. Her son is an Engineer and employed yet teaches in an institution to establish himself and here were these youngsters who desired to grow wealthier in a jiffy with no second thoughts for the victims in this state of affairs. Does technological advancement and growth of a nation mean a lax in values? Honesty is a conviction, an integrity which must have been fostered in all individuals and spruced in adults. The soreness on Mrs Varghese's face in actuality revealed an agonizing contemporary world as we bid goodnight to each other.

30

A Thoughtful Revelation

"Perception of disability lies in the mind" A P J Kalam

He was fair, short, emaciated, wearing slackly appropriate clothes and had black glasses on his eyes for protection. You are right in your presumption; he had undergone a cataract operation. He was standing out side the office chatting amicably to others. I understood that he was the caretaker. We entered the office of Nachiketa Bal Gram, a home for the destitute children after crossing the narrow road on the Gurudwara lane at Akurdi in Pune. There were a few more elderly men who were chatting in the open yard of the orphanage. The place was large, well kept and spotless. The building was tinted yellow with blue doors and windows which were in good form. The office was a tiny space with a table and three chairs with space just adequate for these. We went in to take our seats. My friend has adopted the dependability of two children at Nachiketa. The intention of our visit was that my friend wanted to arrange a workshop by an eminent group for these kids and her sister wanted to teach Indian Classical Music for the concerned children. My friend introduced me to the caretaker who had a smiling countenance. This radiance must have been a reflection of the meaningful life he led. Just opposite to the office was a kitchen which was orderly and hygienic. Dishes and glasses had been stacked neatly. There were a few ladies who were busy cooking the afternoon meal. The caretaker told my friend that she needed to seek permission from the higher authorities for the workshop and the Music classes. He handed her a card with the telephone numbers of the concerned authorities. Later we enquired about the kids. He said that the preparations for getting back to the school after vacations were going on. While departing my friend said that behind the cheerful countenance of the caretaker was a heart-rending story. The caretaker had lost his wife and was living with his married sons. A few years later both the sons refused to shoulder his responsibility. He was left at an old age home where he felt worthless and dejected. His uselessness taught him to transform his life into a significant one for the desolate. He told my friend that he found great solace in being a part and parcel of Nachiketa and would never return back home. He would work at the orphanage till the end of his life. He said that he had also instructed the authorities to deny his funeral rites to his children after his bereavement. He never let his children know about his whereabouts. My admiration for the caretaker augmented because he had resorted to spread joy in the lives of the orphans though he had been forsaken by his own children. Here was a striking person known for his deeds through his necessity of having his own family. Tough times test the worst instincts in people and a very few are able to conduct themselves with respect and control their lives specifically when there is a terrible blow given by a dear one. Shaping our lives in such adversities by paving paths to public service is the most honourable way of displaying belief in oneself. He had focussed his energies to overcome the flaws in life.

31

An Expedition: One step in the path of Edification

As I kept the book "Positive Discipline" aside, memories deluged and everything seemed as if it had transpired recently. It was a rainy day, the morning attendance time for the class. I had begun with the prayer as the school assembly was cancelled. I noticed a couple standing at the doorway with their daughter. I gestured them to wait as I completed the prayer and led myself towards the doorway. The parents told me that she was admitted in class eight. I acknowledged being the class teacher. I glanced at the girl who was a little plump and short with two plaits, immaculately dressed. Her mother longed to speak something more but decided not to. I smiled at the girl who was looking at me predisposed. I took her aside and asked her to introduce herself to the class as usual. She declined. I made her sit in the first row as I always did to make the child feel at home. Since that day she sat on the same bench at the same place and refused to move according to the rotation of seats. She was mischievous and naughty like any other child. Each day the girls would complain about her misbehaviour but she would look at me forlornly as if she were not at fault. One day she fell down in the playground and that was the day I realized that she suffered from epilepsy. "It was a fall in the childhood which caused this misery", said the parent. Within two days she was back to her normal self. By now she had adapted herself to the class. She was meticulous in her work, listened carefully, marked every important aspect and had the seriousness of any gifted child but unfortunately she never retained information in the exams. She could only remember when the clues were given. Hence she did well in the English paper. When I would approve others of their performance in the exam she would raise her hand and I would approve her efforts too. She loved it and would carry a beaming smile throughout the day. The class moved to standard nine and I moved as their class teacher. The strength of the class increased and it was now divided into two sections but she was with me. She was dependable in the day to day happenings much more than I was. She would remind me of the absentees, the homework given, the money to be collected for various activities. She was forever there to hand over a pencil, pen or scissors lacking in my pouch. When she would get tired playing in the hot sun she would rush back to the class where I preferred sitting when the class was empty to complete my work. She could run the smart board and surf activities. In all ways she appeared normal but she could never commit to memory in the exam. I encouraged the virtues she held. Gradually every one began liking her as I would proclaim that she was my favourite. Initially it was to save her from those who oppressed her but progressively she actually turned out to be my preferred. Her eyes spoke volumes about her. During the annual day celebrations she was contented with her role but wanted to dance. Her parents were pleased with her progress. We moved to class tenth and were closer now. I could see her grow more confident. At times when I would admonish her then I could see the agony in her eyes. I would quickly change the tone and tell her my work pressures as a cause and she would smile reassuringly. She would brief me about the class whenever she met me and the class would look at her menacingly but my smile would comfort them. The class had to opt for the boards as we did not have standard 11th in the school and she appeared for it courageously. I rummaged for her result praying God that she should clear the exam but she turned out to be the only one for improvement. I felt a dull pain within me. On contacting the Board they said that she needed to appear for the improvement exam. I knew that ten improvement exams would not bring the desired change in her performance. The last time when I met her, I saw her withdrawn and reluctant to meet me. Her mother brought her to me after a lot of coaxing. I spoke to her reassuring her of the strengths she had and looked deep into her eyes. There was anxiety and dismay which I could never expunge from my mind. Over the years of togetherness, she understood me better. Somewhere I felt I had lost the trust and faith a student cherishes in the teacher. Her disappointment had let down the teacher in me.

32

A POSITIVE APPROACH

"Perfection is such an unrealistic expectation which is discouraging too for those who feel they must live up to an adult's expectation of perfection" Jane Nelson

Winter mornings are gloomy and frosty at Durga Tekdi, a man made forest which has got its name due to the Durga temple on the hills. No one likes to discard the warmth of a blanket to hustle for a morning walk into a dingy dark forest where you see ethereal human figures till the sun rises to illuminate the beings around. As habitual we reached the outskirts of the forest area, parked the car and started walking briskly to overcome the chill. While walking along the long stretch guiding the walking track in the forest we felt warmth enliven us. We could see many vehicles parked in the parking lot. The cars were sheltered in the huge ground and the scooters and bikes along the core path.

Outlying the main gate at the entrance a striking long log is mounted vertically on two forked logs on either sides forming a barrier which indicates people to evade parking their scooters and cars beyond the point. We love walking the whole stretch despite the fact that the inside walk is nearly three kms uphill. It is an exotic scenic spot where there are tiny green spaces lined by hedges with metallic benches for weary travellers. There are sheltered rounded paved spots at various spots on both the sides of the walking track interspersed between the fast growing trees. It is enthralling to watch the sky change hues at sunrise as the red ball of fire makes its existence through the murky sky boasting mingled colours.

At a distance behind me I could hear a girl whining as she desperately wanted to go back home. It was Diwali vacation and many of the parents trudged their children by ousting them from sleep to keep up the continuity of their walks. I turned back to see a father with a twelve year old daughter cross by. The girl was amused as her father had tricked her into walking with a few engrossing exercises making her forget the long path. The girl felt delighted on her achievement of completing the long walk. Through out the vacation the father had something special to narrate to the daughter. They would race uphill or down the terrain. When the school began there was a lull in the forest with only the older folks rushing back home to send their children to school. I love to dash down the last stretch. Yesterday as I began to run I heard footsteps following me and then overtake me. I saw that it was the little girl. I kept at pace and saw that she raced beyond the gate reached the log of wood and jumped across using the log as a hurdle, a clean jump. She later reached the car and waited for her father to reach with a gleam of pride. Subtle and gentle coaxing had led to this accomplishment. It reminded me that gentle cajoling in any path of life with the intention of encouraging always leads to multitude in results

"Recognition of improvement is encouraging and inspires children to continue their efforts. A positive approach invites co operation, mutual respect, responsibility and social interest." Jane Nelson

33

JUSTIFICATION OF LIFE

'Happiness is not a place where you reach but a state which you create' –Robin Sharma

It was mid May summer evening. I was waiting for my friend in the garden area which is a part of a multiple building blocks. I heard loud noises of children running in the central park around the godly figurines, rejoicing, their prattle and laughter demonstrating the happiness they felt during summer vacation. Far away I saw a mother followed by her little daughter, holding a writing pad in her hand and a school bag on her shoulder, the mother seemed annoyed while the little girl sported a sore expression on her face. The child's thoughts were focused elsewhere as she followed her mother. The child may not have been more than three years old so it perplexed me more. These days we find children going for guidance to tutors throughout their growing years of schooling so often that when a child refuses to go for extra classes, the mother worries as to how a child would cope up with the extra burden of tuitions when the child grows up without habituating the routine. On asking the little girl's mother, I came to know that the mother was sending her daughter for a practice in handwriting so that her future would be brighter in the coming years. The child came back within no time as the teacher seemed to be absent from her duty. The delight, the child, felt showed her detest for the classes, but now the mother walked away anxiously planning her child's future. It sent a dull pain within me when I remembered having done this to my little boy who wanted to play, but my goal was to grow him to face the society rather than ascertain his happiness. Over the years, I have understood that people forgo little joys and thrills of life while pursuing larger goals of societal prospects which perhaps stand for momentary stature. I also understood that happiness differs from person to person. A poor person finds happiness in owning basic needs like food and shelter, a rich person finds contentment in showing wealth and status off, a spiritual person finds peace in contentment concerned with minimum needs while a child finds pleasure in any situation, being completely unmindful to the walk and talk of society.

Recently I discovered a new park in one of localities nearby with a walking track and a huge lawn area with swings and slides for kids. It has benches for the elderly and young. It is well maintained, wide open, and a person can view all around the park as they are walking. It is well lit in the nights too. There I saw these three young boys who might have been twelve years old, they sat huddled together on a bench, a two liter bottle of soft drink was tucked in between the space left. They had two packs of potato wafers; they relished each bite of it with a sip of the soft drink. They were overjoyed and enjoyed their party. I have never seen this kind of joy in a child who gets this often savor it so.

There was a mother who would not stop smiling after her little child landed down the slide all alone. There were ladies chatting, the old feeling complacent for having grown old and a young couple arguing endlessly. Each day we stumble on numerous ways of being happy and thankful, but each day we also ascertain millions of ways to be miserable and discontented. A child has the innocence to forget the difficulties and celebrate the joys in life, but adulthood often lands us in self pity and lament. I remember my school days when I felt contented reading borrowed books and comics in the summer evenings, the smell of the pages still lingers within me. A good book, playing marbles with my brother and sisters, eating watermelon late in the evenings accompanied by narrations by my parents about their childhood days, building sand castles on the hard soil kept me happy. I never aspired for anything more for my heart had the purity of thoughts. Many a times accomplishment leaves no room for a childlike virtuousness in enjoying an ecstasy of an early morning sunrise, the sunset, dew drops on leaves or large and tiny rain drops, frosty winter mornings or the beautiful flowers in spring. Many a time we leave the world contributing nothing for the needy, helping none by being over involved in our growth and opulence making one repent when death approaches. Resolving to lead a satisfied and serene life by being a part of life with the purpose of doing well for others will help us leave the world majestically with no misgivings.

'Life is no brief candle for me. It is a sort of splendid torch which I want to make it burn as brightly as possible before handing it on to future generations'- George Bernard Shaw

34

THE CHOICE OF ANSWERABILITY

"The price of greatness is responsibility." — Winston Churchill

The stream of water emerged out in a jet and surged ten feet above us. It was breathtaking to watch it in the backdrop of a spherical red glowing sun rising in the blue canopy interspersed with clouds. The underbridge that connects Pradhikaran and Ravet has open space on both the sides of the road. A water pipe had burst on the side that leads to Pradhikaran. It was early in the morning, and there was an early morning walker who was admiring the panorama. Looking at the jet of water we stopped for a while, and decided to go to the office of the municipal water authority in PCMC to report the gushing eruption of water. The office is a little away from the place we live. On reaching the office, we found the road leading the office was sandy with pebbles strewn all over the path leading towards the entrance of the building, but the gates were thrown open. We saw a security seated on a chair with his eyes half closed, his forehead covered with a handkerchief in the form of a cap. A few more people were loitering inside, when we gestured the security to come out as we were finding it difficult to move in with me as a pillion rider. The security, a relaxed person, gestured back. While we were getting ready to enter, there appeared a person on his bike. He seemed a little more involved in the job. We quickly narrated about the jet of water. The man looked at us pensively and asked us the exact location. He did not ask us about the intensity of the leak but questioned us about the exact location of the leak repeatedly.We described the spot, but it looked as if he was interested only in knowing the location. Finally, his eyes sparkled as he said that the other side, where the water pipe was conked out, was not under their jurisdiction. By now my husband got annoyed and said that they could call the authorities and report the leak' as water was getting wasted and that it was the sense of duty to look into these matters irrespective of the location. The incident reminded me of several instances when an individual rubs out accountability on others.

My friend had lost her pouch at the vegetable vendor's shop close to her house. She told the vendor to return the documents and that he could keep the money in the purse but the vendor seemed adamant in acknowledging the fact. The pouch contained her driving license and her bank ATM card. She got in touch with bank authorities and blocked her card and reported the loss of her licence to the road transport authorities who asked her to get a Xerox copy of the lost licence and get a FIR filed in the local police station. She rushed to the police station in Pradhikaran to get a letter, to hasten the process of getting her licence back. They asked her the address of her residence, and impulsively said that the area was under the jurisdiction of the Dehu Road police station, which is nearly ten km away. Many of the people felt it was better to pay some money to driving school authorities and get a licence. When the police verification for our passport was carried out, we went to the Chinchwad police station. After completing the authentication, they said that we need another verification at the DehuRoad police station as we have lived in the present area for less than a year and that the earlier residence in Nigdi came under the jurisdiction of the other police station.

The beautiful University campus has dried plants at various spots, perhaps it is because of the variable responsibility of watering the plants. Over the years I have experienced this shifting responsibility in all the quarters of life, very often because an individual is a coward to accept the liability or the lapse. They say that any nation flourishes with accountable citizens, but people dread accountability. Many a times when they encounter an accident victim, lying neglected on the road, they are indecisive in admitting the victim in a hospital as the accompanier would be tormented with the registration of a case and a series of back up visits. Even when a vehicle lost is registered many trips have to be made to the court spending more money than the loss.

Many a times the most responsible in the society, the educationists fail to take up the responsibility of the failure of their students as a failure means a lack of interest in the student that is in fact, the failure of the teacher, but the culpability is shifted very easily on the parent. A parent shifts the blameworthiness back on the teacher and the blame game continues. Every day we find people taking pleasure in this ridiculous shifting accountability instead of shouldering or sharing a responsibility.

A keen sense of commitment to a cause without an expectation for rewards transforms the inner strengths through an awareness to be an accountable and answerable person in societal transformation.

"It is wrong and immoral to seek to escape the consequences of one's acts." — Mahatma Gandhi

35

DIVERSITY

"I think... if it is true that there are as many minds as there are heads, then there are as many kinds of love as there are hearts." — Leo Tolstoy, Karenina,

It was quarter past two; I was late and feared entering the hall. Golay hall in the English department of the University was closed with the outer wooden door clamped. I desperately wished to attend the presentation though the topic was on a comparative study on Multiculturalism by Dr Dorothy from Georgia State University. I missed the foreword for having been late. I saw a young girl probably in her post graduation just pull the door wide open; I thanked God and this youngster as I sneaked in to the hall behind her. I sat on the nearest seat near the door in the most uncomfortable way but felt happy that the visit which is twenty two km away from home did not go vain. Dr. Dorothy stood there and was deeply engrossed presenting her Paper. She wore a

126

salwar kameez with the dupatta loosely thrown across her shoulder, she seemed middle aged with a few strands of black haired locks near the forehead, rest of her hair grey. She was tall,fair and brawny. The hall was filled with students pursuing post-graduation, M.Phil and PhD in English. We all listened to her deeply.

The word '*Multiculturalism*' relates to communities containing multiple cultures. The term is used to describe either cultural diversity or the demography of a specific place, sometimes at the organizational level like schools, businesses, nations. She also spoke in context to post colonialism. She referred to anthologies or the collected works. I was looking at her trying to imbibe everything including the way she presented the paper. It was time for clarification then. She looked around as she sipped mineral water. She seemed tired due to the heat yet was wholehearted. The hall had grown hotter but the air conditioners were working. Students asked her elaborate questions and she answered it in her best way. She spoke about the writers and about the critics and everything related. It was a learning period for me. Our head of the Dept Dr. Raja Rao finally proclaimed that there was time for just another question but there were two hands up. A Kashmiri student put his question. I looked at him, kashmiris are considered to be a minority group in our country. I realised that I was also a minority in Maharashtra but then where did I belong to? I am a Konkani from Goa,well that was what my father had told me, but my native place is Kerala, have been brought up in Hyderabad, and have been living in Maharashtra for more than two decades. Then am I a minority in Maharashtra?

It reminded me of the incident when I was working for a school in Mumbai. A kindergarten student was run over by a mini bus, the driver failed to see the little girl standing on the road. My friend threw her bag, picked the child and ran to the doctor in a bid to save the life of the little girl. Her dress was soaked in blood but she could think nothing other than the child. The doctors tried to revive the little girl but had to declare her dead. The mother who had come to pick this little girl had swooned on seeing the accident. Still later she was brought to reality. Many days later the mother came to school and thanked my friend for the timely act which had helped them reconcile to the destiny thinking that their little one was attended by doctors who had tried to revive her and that God had destined this. My friend was a Keralite and the child was a Maharashtrian.

I wished to ask Dorothy that the literature, dialect and cultures differ but still there is something which bonds us and the literature. I knew the answer as I had heard Dorothy speak about brotherhood. I was reminded of empathy in Shakespeare's 'Venus and Adonis', Jataka tales portraying Buddhist morality and Jewish literature like zeemach's 'It Could be Worse' that literature bonds us through its universal values by reliving the readers of emotions and perhaps evoking powerful emotions. We are bonded by the morals and the malevolence of Humanity.

"It is time for parents to teach young people early on that in diversity there is beauty and there is strength."
— Maya Angelou

36

LESSONS LEARNT

"Life isn't about finding yourself. Life is about creating yourself." George Bernard Shaw

He trailed behind me as I entered the gate, into the campus, up the stairs. Hastily, I rushed into the library. He paused at the doorway, and moved into the corridor, I peeped to watch him quiver along the stairs which led to the other sections in the Arts building of Pune University. He seemed young, perhaps he was in his twenties but lacked the ability to coordinate his body movements. I returned the library books and came back only to find him outside the building in the dried woods where the cars are parked. I ran and got into the car and looked at him fearfully, but he did not see me, he rushed back into the building again with the same look on his face, searching for what he had forgotten. His body pulled him apart and hurled him to another place in spite of his organised thoughts. Perhaps he was challenging life for the demands which had left him without the most basic essential in life, coordination of movements.

She looked into the tank lovingly and told me there were four little turtles. I could see only one in it. There was a small water spout through which water trickled into a hollow place in the tank. She told me there was a shy turtle in the hollow place. When the water level rose I could see a very tiny turtle. I looked at her. She was constantly gazing at the turtle, there was a serenity as she spoke softly with immense love for the animal. I looked around the sprawling space filled with greenery, impeccably kept with a variety of plants. She told me that her in laws too had loved the place and would walk barefooted on the large lawn area. I felt they were blessed to have this tranquil place. I asked her whether leaving the place would pain her. She smiled and said bravely that they had lived and enjoyed the beauty for two whole years and that being a part of the Indian Army had taught her the art of relinquishing with ease. This was Brig. S P Goswami's house at Pune. The soft spoken person was his wife, Mrs. Rashmi Goswami, whom I was meeting for the first time personally and since they were leaving Pune it was the last time. Brig Goswami had been the Chairman of the school where I had worked, we shared the same ideals and principles in the field of Education. I wanted to meet him once before they left for Delhi, he invited me home. I dreaded visiting him at home assuming it would be a very formal one but since I wanted to meet him, I went at the planned time, surprisingly it turned out to be a very unceremonious and pleasurable visit. While returning back I exclaimed about the well kept garden when they took us around. Me and my husband admired their modesty and above all an example of credibility through words and deeds for people, the ones who had worked with them and those like me who no longer worked for them.They viewed their troubles as blessings determining their disposition through experiences while discovering the richness of their internal strength.

It was early in the morning, the men in the shacks and shanties were rolling the aluminium sheets and getting ready to leave the place. They tugged the sheets and rolled it, packed their suitcases and bags with their sparse belongings. They had lived here for more than a year building five building blocks with seven storeys each, and now the work was more or less complete. The builder was transporting them to a new place to begin building a new complex. They seemed happy while leaving the place and their half built homes. The new residents of the complex did not miss them nor acknowledged their role in building their homes while they remained homeless. Giving up for these uneducated daily wage laborers was as easy as a saint though they were spiritually neglectful.

These few incidents taught me numerous lessons to lead a bountiful life. The young lad with a lack of coordination of body movements taught me to lead a life with calculated risks rather than letting life move away in regret and misery. It taught me to experience pain and relish joy.

My visit to Brig S P Goswami's house taught me a lesson of letting go things effortlessness for life is incredible and bounteous when you believe things for what they are and appreciate its true meaning in God's ways

The ease of letting go things as daily wage labourers taught me to recognise a change as an opportunity, leading a rewarded and actualised life, rather than a defeat while detaching oneself from outcomes.

-Strength does not come from physical capacity. It comes from an indomitable will. Mahtma Gandhi

37

MINDFULNESS

'Thoughts control your world, be a firm guardian of
your thought, make certain it is of the highest quality'
-Robin Sharma

The little boy was engrossed in a sheer joy of his
highhandedness over a bird on the tree. He was
seated on his bicycle, with his neck craned upwards, his
mouth opened and closed as a crow's beak as he made
strange caw, cah sounds. It looked like a crow on the
tree had befriended the little boy as it cawed back. The
boy cawed again, the bird looked down and cawed at
him, both were deeply involved in their chat, it was a
breathtaking sight with the boy basking in the morning
sun rays. None of the by passers watched him. A few
morning walkers come for their walk, regularly, but
many a times it looks as if the exercise is a troublesome
task. Many use the opportunity to gossip destroying the
serenity of a walk with their anxious high-pitched talk.

A few others have earphones stuffed in their ears, leading them into artificial environs where they are unable to hear the chirping of the sparrows, squeaking of squirrels, twitter of the hummingbird or the bees humming. A few others concentrate on their physical disability rather than the splendour of nature, but this little boy was deriving immense pleasure while being emotionally attached to the bird, a sensitivity to nature.

In the evening the hot winds had caused the cooler currents of air to blow vigorously, it transformed the weather, the dark grey clouds wafted in, and were about to precipitate inspiring children to trickle out of their flats to the garden area. It drizzled and still later rained moderately, children leapt in joy, savoured rain and played in totality of a mindfulness. In the neighbouring balcony I saw a mother seething with worry and anger as her kids capered and soared in the downpour, and plunged in the puddles. Far off they heard the shrill sounds of their anxious mothers, but ignored it, for the joy of rain in the hot weather is something beyond heavens. The young girls ran hither thither, while junior boys walked gradually getting drenched discussing the outer space and Universe, the adolescents played cricket while the girls looked on, but my ardour and feelings were with the very little kids who went crazy waddling in the water, thumping their feet, raising their skirts and jumping and vaulting in the small pools of water.They knew only the sheer bliss of rain. I felt sorry for my neighbour who had relinquished the magnificence of nature through her apprehensiveness for her kids.

I remembered the Kuchipudi Dance classes run by Ms Swapna Chilla for the young and the old. While learning this classical style I understood that whenever our mind goes astray, we miss a hold on the dance step. When our teacher performs these dance steps, we ape at her in admiration. She told us that the mind, thoughts and actions are linked and that Dance movements or the 'rasa' are best portrayed as a reflection of our thoughts and actions and our presence, all synchronous.

Many a time careers are chosen without a curiosity, this leads to a feeling of annoyance, often this exasperation is meted out as anger. There are cases when a doctor creates an impact among his patients right in the beginning of his career. I still remember Dr. Yadav who ran helter-skelter to find what my ailment was and did not rest till the reports confirmed what I had. She turned into our family doctor from that instant, never to be forgotten to this day.

Once while walking on the treadmill, my mind wandered, I slipped, it was lucky that I could hold onto one of the bars, to escape the calamity.

A few years back, while returning home from my work I saw a display of artefacts, they were made of teak wood arranged on a clearing along the Mumbai Pune highway; I was eyeing it for a long time as I was driving. I never knew when I slipped off the main road and fell down in the hedges on the road side. The passers by lifted me and I slowly drove back home wiser.

Many a times a job, a deed even a charitable act rebounds because of the lack of mindfulness. Mindfulness is a state when we are energetic and are aware of the present, rather than the past or future. This mindfulness

Jyothi Ramesh Pai

helps remarkably in lowering the stress caused due to worry and creates an overall wellness because it can be used anytime and can quickly bring lasting results as one is aware of his or her thoughts and feelings.

'As the physically weak man can make himself strong by careful patient training, so the weak man of weak thoughts can make them strong by exercising himself in right thinking'

38

INNER PEACE, THE
SECRET OF HAPPINESS

"A joy that's shared is a joy made double." John Ray

We were at Pune railway station half an hour ahead of time. We got the platform tickets and climbed the access ramp to reach the over head bridge from where we were directed to platform number five. We reached the platform and found it reasonably full. There were people every where, a mail train to Bangalore was about to depart the platform. We lingered as it slowly chugged and stirred ahead. The crowd did not budge instead there were many more people trickling slowly to board the Mumbai Hyderabad express. There was a huge family with their extended family of roughly fifteen people with kids and adults on a holiday. The women were clad in "burkha" a black cloak. We were frantically searching for a place to be on our feet with out people pushing us around. We were to meet my sisters who had boarded the train from Mumbai.

As time went by people started hastening with their luggage and families. There were a few young girls sluggishly walking around, towing their luggage in oblivion. There was yet another family with two kids, the younger one bawling away when his mother wanted him to wear slippers. There were two elderly ladies very well dressed with their decently clothed husbands chatting in low voices displaying the kind of poise needed. The loud voice of the railway schedule announcer assured us that the train was on time. Everyone heaved a sigh of relief. The platform was dirtier than ever with people spitting, bits of papers of goodies flying around which had been callously thrown. In the hub dub there was a guava vendor who was selling guavas. A peanut seller was wandering in search of a place with a coir woven stool and his basket of peanuts. Two young boys hastily bought it and gulped it down their throat. Books and magazines were being brought by people to recline and enjoy reading during their travel. We looked on waiting for the train to arrive. It had turned hotter with the sun's scorching rays agonizing me more than ever. I detested the grime around, the horde of people, the mushy smell and would have scampered away but for the dinner I had painfully cooked for my sisters so that they could have home made food. Suddenly cold wind started blowing; it turned dark and cloudy, and began pouring. People began cursing their fate as it had turned muddy with water trickling, reaching their baggage. There was no space to move under the shade. And then it began pouring heavily. I was muttering under my breath and was terribly upset. I raised my head to see water gushing through over head pipes which lined the roof top of the platform. The water was mucky as it flowed through the dusty roof tops. As I stood wondering what next, I saw two little boys in unclean set of clothes. They looked like those children who sweep up the compartment and beg money as compensation. They were yelling and hastily unbuttoning their shirts. They ran with the shirt now in their hands under the water which was pouring from the roof top and began bathing gladly. They didn't have soap or any such luxuries. They hopped, leaped and shrieked in the happiness of having cooled their bodies. Later they thumped their shirts on the floor in water and wringed it, it was their way of washing clothes, plastered their hair back and went to the railway canteen to relish some food. We lead a comfortable life but a few minutes in the filth and mob pained us. These little boys who were combating their fate with a valiant heart above all the miseries in life could search happiness in little things like a thunder shower reminding us of Swami Vivekananda who said

"Happiness presents itself before man, wearing the crown of sorrow on its head. He who welcomes it must also welcome sorrow".

39

SALUTE THE SPIRIT, HOMAGE

Jessie covered her hands tightly around her bent knees; her head slumped as she gaped elsewhere. She didn't recognize the alteration of twilight into the crack of dawn. She had a woebegone expression and looked out apathetically. She had aroused early in fact she had not slept a wink last night. She and her sister Nancy consoled each other but some happenings cannot be over and done so easily. Nancy envisaged how blissful they were a few months back. Nancy was my close friend and a colleague, who resided at Nallasopara west with her sister. Both were married and owned two apartments in the same housing block. Their spouses were employed in Saudi Arabia and so would visit once or twice in a year. They belonged to Mangalore and spoke Konkani. They lived in Nancy's flat and had sub-let Jessie's flat. Mumbai is a metropolis of dreams and people state it is the grace of Mahalakshmi and Haji Ali which contributes to prosperity. Jessie worked at Church Gate for a multinational company.

In the year 1993 a special train catering suburban services called ladies special train had begun for women and children below twelve. It plied in the peak hours in the morning and evening for the office goers from Virar to Church gate. Women attuned their timings to embark this train as it was comfortable and secure than the ordinary train. The usual local trains encompass two second class ladies compartments and a first class compartment for women. These are by and large jampacked in the peak hours and boarding a compartment common for all meant giving lease to pervasive minds who abuse women. Jessie loved boarding the ladies special train in the morning from Nallasopara and in the evening at six from church gate. It had become a part of most of the women travelling this stretch. Husbands, fathers and brothers were assured of the well being of their women, and they would never try to hasten them to amend their schedule. It was a dreary cold day, must have been in the month of December 1993, the weather conditions changed significantly and a rainstorm raged, displacing lives, uprooting trees, dismantling electrical wires. The ladies special train chugged and halted a little away from the yard in Borivali. Due to the storm and black out it had turned pitch dark. Tenuously they could see a few lights. Although there were many women they were despondent with the proceedings. It was growing darker; suddenly the audacious ones persuaded the timid ones to leap out and move to the station as they could board a different train. There are numerous railway tracks at Borivali. They began crossing the tracks. Jessie was in one of the compartments, she considered the decision.

After reflecting she persuaded a friend and went back from the doorway to pick her bag and was about to leap out when she heard an annihilating sound of bodies being slaughtered. She froze as she saw another local train without headlight moving silently had run over the women who were crossing the tracks. The train came to a stand still but more than sixty bodies were lying on the tracks lifeless, battered, beyond recognition. Blackouts in Mumbai are for a very short while, lights were restored but lives mislaid. Jessie didn't know whether she should have rejoiced and thanked God for saving her own life or feel sorry for the deceased. She clamoured through the crowd and reached home. She didn't want to travel by the local train. When I met Nancy at the station the next day she narrated the loss. She looked at me beseechingly. She did not have the courage to board the train. I was alarmed, so was she. We held our hands as we noticed the local train approaching the station and gradually boarded it. Life moved on. People voiced their opinion against the Railways. Compensation was paid to the families of the departed. We saw Jessie a few days later, she had begun working and life changed despite the sorrow. This episode is a salutation to the spirits of the people of Mumbai who are determined, valiant and strongly believe that miracles do happen in the lives of individuals who lay their trust in God who dispels darkness and fills delight in their lives.

40

PENSIONERS' PARADISE

"Learning is an ornament in prosperity, a refuge in adversity, and a provision in old age." — Aristotle

The Bank was an undersized one situated in a huge open place in the most picturesque surrounding. Across the road were a beautiful garden and an open restaurant. On one side was the Volkswagen showroom. This Bank is situated on the road leading to National Chemical Laboratory near Pashan. It was crammed with people. The employees across the counters were snatching a break to drink water to wet their parched throats as they answered and directed people. The guard was watching everyone cautiously and answering the queries put by the tired customers. My husband tugged me along though I was not very interested being there. I stood near the gateway hoping he would finish his work soon. He has taken up all these responsibilities hence I felt naive as I looked around the transactions going on. There were many notes of notice put up. One which caught my attention was a notice put for pensioners. It asked the pensioners to provide a living certificate with a copy of their Pan Card and other certificates. It was amusing that a person needed to provide evidence for his existence to claim his pension. I observed that there were many old people in the bank. It was pitiable to see many of the old couples slowly winding their way to the bank. In spite of the desire to serve people at the earliest it seemed to be a Herculean task for the authorities.

Then I saw a van which looked like a locker safe which was accompanied by two police authorities who carried a gun each. They stood cautiously as the bank official opened the door of the van followed by a grill door. The bank employee went in and brought a metallic suitcase with a lock. He closed all the doors and walked into the bank to a covert corner. At the end there were two counters called the green counters which had been well decorated. On inquiring, I came to know that these counters were like a mini ATM. I strained to read the functions when I saw a man sitting over there gazing a lady. He was seated and gaped at a lady standing near the counter. The lady walked away detesting his looks. The man gave the impression of being inquisitive about his surroundings. The bank employees came again with a larger suitcase and the police man following. It diverted my attention back to the door as they started loading the suitcase in the van again. Out of the blue I saw an old lady drag the old man towards the door. The old man walked like a little child. At the doorway he paused uncertainly. The lady got down on the step outside the door and coaxed him to get down. He stepped down cautiously and smiled gleefully. She then hauled him to a pole and left him holding the pole and then went to a counter to get the passbook updated. The man grasped the pole and behaved like a little boy glancing here and there, never leaving his hand for the fear of falling down. When the lady concluded her work, he held on to her like a child does to his mother.

Slowly they walked out reminding me of the second childishness in man. I understood the person was undergoing a neuromuscular disorder. He looked at people unassumingly but people misread him. The lady had brought this old man along with her to collect his pension. It was dismal that the man who had earned the pension no longer understood what it meant now. It was wonderful that he provided his family a livelihood despite his shortcomings.

"Cherish all your happy moments: they make a fine cushion for old age." — Christopher Morley

41

THE JOYFUL PRESENT

They say 'Shared grief is half the sorrow, but happiness when shared, is doubled.'

There was just one pair of medium sized ladies leather slippers left. The hawker shrieked at the top of his voice soliciting people to buy it. I and my friend had reached the place wandering and now both of us wanted the pair. We asked the vendor for another pair. The vendor glimpsed at us and nodded in disapproval. The whole ground and the surrounding area in Neemuch was covered with young scouts and guides in the age group of 13 to 15. It was a State Rally for the scouts and guides. We belonged to K V Golconda No 1 situated in Hyderabad but all the scouts and guides from various Kendriya Vidyalayas at Hyderabad and Secunderabad were included in Mumbai region.

From K V Golconda near about ten students belonging to class ninth had been chosen to represent the State rally. We belonged to different sections. I and my friend Rupa belonged to the C section. My mother never wanted me to be a part of this rally. She had pampered me being the youngest and I honestly did not know the basics of being independent even in my day to day chores. As a neighbour was going for this trip she reluctantly let me go when my father stupendously decided to let me go. The Rally was organised in the month of December at Neemuch which lies on the border of Rajasthan. When we reached Neemuch after two and a half days travel in a passenger train we found our accommodation was in mere canvas tents. We had to settle down fast with our luggage as we had to display our mastered skills with reef knots and many other skills. There were many tests to be dealt and endurance tests to be endured; the greatest one was sleeping in the cold tents. Each day was a suffering of waking up at five in the morning and rushing for the parade.

It was a harsh period and we all missed the warmth of our homes and our parents and siblings. Deep within my heart I decided never to leave my home. It was during a bio break that we all had loitered to eat cream rolls sold by the villagers in a make shift shop. There was a day left to wind up. We all were on the look out to buy a few things for our parents.

I bought a few trinkets for my sisters and a painting for my brother as we made way towards the man selling these chappals. Both of us wanted to buy it for our mothers. The vendor had only one pair. I didn't know the size of my mother's foot.

Rupa seemed to have an idea. The vendor quoted rupees ten but we haggled and brought the price down to rupees nine. They were crudely made by the villagers who carried these in a basket. Rupa said that her mother would be pleased but she let me take it after a little introspection. We completed the training successfully and surpassed as first class guides. On reaching home my mother got busy disinfecting all my things. At the end of the day I gave away the gifts to my sisters and brother. When I showed the chappals to my mother, she lovingly hugged me and enquired why had I not spent the money on myself. Before I could say anything she wiped her tears from the corner of her eyes saying that any other child would have spent the money to buy goodies. I felt tall that day due to the appreciation attained and the happiness experienced by my mother. I lost my mother the very next year but have always cherished the memory of giving her a present. If my friend had taken the pair of chappals for her mother that day, I would have had the remorse of not endowing my mother with a gift in her lifetime. As I grew older I learnt a valuable lesson of giving and living with the most joyful gift "the present", the precious present. If you want to feel rich, just count all the things you have that money can't buy.

'Today is a gift that is why it is called The Present.'
Dedicated to my friend Rupa Mukherjee

42

COMPASSION AGAINST EXPECTATION

Rohan looked tenderly at his distressed teacher and told her that he was not hungry. He said that he suffered from colitis and so he felt better when he did not eat. He did not have an appetite and suffered from nausea. His teacher gazed mystified at the behaviour. Rohan was compliant, bright, diligent and above all well mannered and courteous, an apple of the teacher's eye. Rohan a fourteen years old was lean and lanky. A healthy boy with a positive attitude. Adolescence is a period of rapid growth and when Rohan was indifferent to consumption of food, his teacher was apprehensive.

She hastily skimmed through the dictionary as she was an economics teacher and words like colitis sounded Greek and Latin.

Accordingly she understood that colitis was the inflammation and sores of the colon accompanied by bleeding and pus in the large intestine. She read that the specific cause was unheard of but could be caused due to emotional distress. It is caused in people with an abnormal immune system but the reason is unclear. It pained her but she was sure that Rohan had got this ailment due to the fretfulness caused by the separation of his parents. At first Rohan's was a joint family with his grand parents living with them. It was an emotionally unwavering home with a wonderfully accomplished grandson Rohan.

As years went by Rohan's parents got separated due to mutual consent. His mother was posted at Mumbai and so his father took care of him. He managed his needs to his best but Rohan's lunch was a huge endeavour as his parents had gone back to the village. Rohan was a mature child who never let his pangs of hunger known to his father. He at times felt it was better to stay with his mother who had no one else other than Rohan. He missed the affection of his mother and the scrumptious food she cooked. Many a times he would not have his lunch and so felt the strong shooting pain of hunger. He found his teacher a great source of solace. His teacher was a Gandhian who believed in the principle of control of palate which emphasises a restrain on quantity and quality in diet, thought and speech. Rohan knew that his teacher would be at leisure during the lunch break. He would rush to her to chat and forget his troubles thus they grew closer to share Rohan's woes and joys. Rohan many a times craved he had a mother akin to his teacher. A few years back Rohan's mother got a transfer back to Pune and took charge of Rohan. When the initial fervour of caring for Rohan enthused she began neglecting Rohan. She found it difficult managing Rohan. During one of the

Parent teacher meet the teacher warned his mother about Rohan's failing health both bodily and psychologically. It aggrieved the teacher that Rohan was being subjected to an emotional stress with both the parents tossing the child like a neglected pebble. Rohan's parents began afresh with the teacher's advice but God had destined other wise. Rohan had been diagnosed with colitis. He felt better when he did not eat. His teacher was upset as Rohan was a wonderful boy regardless of all the hitches in his life. Rohan earnestly was happy to spend the supplementary time with his teacher as they skipped lunch, one due to spiritual restraint and the other one due to bodily constraints. It was a unique bond of love and compassion against expectation.

> "When we truly love others without condition, without strings, we help them feel secure and safe and validated and affirmed in their essential worth, identity and integrity" Stephen R Covey

43

HUMAN STATURE

"Character cannot be developed in ease and quiet. Only through experience of trial and suffering can the soul be strengthened, vision cleared, ambition inspired, and success achieved." Helen Keller

"Human ego respects a person of stature" It said that a person of stature is respected, valued and the whole world is polite and kind. I wondered what stature was here. I understood that people do not respect any other human being for what the person is but they respect their position, their wealth, their beauty, their power and their achievements and accomplishments.

It suddenly reminded me of my drive to Subrata Roy Sahara Stadium. Subrata Roy Sahara Stadium is a newly built stadium which was inaugurated during the IPL games. We drove to the place searching for a property site which had commenced building a series of apartments on the sprawling grounds near the stadium. The stadium is near to Mumbai Pune highway. The drive was a pleasant one on a winter afternoon. As we were nearing I found the roads growing less crowded and finally we were all alone on the long stretch with tall grass on both the sides of the road. There were two roads ahead with one leading to the site where I could see the weary workers drooling over the unfinished expanse of a new building on the property site. On the other side a little ahead was the stadium standing forlorn and abandoned with not a soul stirring by.

My husband stopped and questioned me as to where I intended to go. Impulsively I pointed towards the road leading to the stadium. I had seen the stadium several times in the evening flood lights as it stood magnificent when we were returning back from Mumbai. I had also witnessed the construction but today the gleam and the appeal was missing but I sought to go in the vicinity of it. My husband drove me straight in to the stadium. He was well versed with the roads due to the presence of a chemical factory whose exports had been looked into as a part of his official duties during his tenure. We finally reached the road leading to the stadium. It was hot with three guards sitting at the gateway. They were perhaps resting. They said there were closed circuit televisions and wouldn't allow us in. We some how managed to convince that we intended to click a couple of photographs. They allowed us and asked us to come back on the 22nd and 23rd of December when the cricket match for Ranjhi trophy would be played. We agreed and came out of another exit to see a part of a village with a crude mud road leading towards the village.

As we kept looking around we saw an old lady carry a lamb in her arms. She was old and a little bent with the hardships of life and aging. I stood and looked at her in admiration. The lamb was heavy but she had the empathy within her to feel for its twinge. I stopped her as I clicked a photograph for the blog. She gave me one of her best beaming smiles. I admired her for what she was as she led a meaningful and an eventful life of benevolence and thoughtfulness for the erstwhile. I was also reminded me of the affluent in our settlement who worked out their dogs lugged to the scooter handle as they ride their scooters. It is an excruciating sight. But here was a villager who in all probability must have been an illiterate with contemplation far beyond the literates and cultured which made her stand apart in significance with positive reception, respect and glory to her stature of human status. It was implicit that it was not the position, splendour or accomplishment but it was the exquisiteness of the character, the deeds of a person which motivates a person respect the other person. I remembered several instances and found that each time I have respected the person with a rich disposition and integrity of conviction.

"Fame is a vapour, popularity an accident, riches take wing, and only character endures."

44

VALOR OR EQUANIMITY

"Being deeply loved by someone gives you strength, while loving someone deeply gives you courage."
— Lao Tzu

The main gate of our building opens on the Rajyog marg, a narrow long lane which leads to the main road on one end and towards Ravet, an upcoming locale on the other end. However the road leading to Ravet is not yet set, it is a muddy path with gravel which has got hardened due to sun's heat and rainwater. The narrow road widens into a large expanse and encompasses a lowland where garbage is dumped, sorted and disseminated to sellers.

This area has a board of Pimpri chinchwad Municipal Corporation stuck in the ground signifying the negligence of the Municipal Authorities. Once we traverse this area we are in Ravet which is full of life with a multitude of shopping arenas, bazaars, eateries, hospitals, Gym and aerobic classes, hardware and grocery shops. The well lit skyscrapers incorporated with their own generators and transformers embrace the well paved long roads speaking of augmentation and development in that area. People enjoy walking and conversing at the shopping arenas and the open air restaurants. It is indeed a lively place. It was around six in the evening. I could see the blue sky change hues of red to shades of grey throwing me into a dilemma of taking the long route to reach Ravet or just walking across the ill maintained road at a stone's throw. I resolved to walk across the kuccha road.

As I passed the low land I met this little girl who must have been no more than twelve years of age. Clad in a salwar kameez with her dupatta tied securely as adults she drove a worn out bicycle. She had a huge bundle of twigs on the back seat. Her face had a charm which made me stop her on a whim. Many a times this stretch is lonely with hooligans driving ruthlessly. There are eve teasers at times and a pack of dogs to keep people at bay. As such most of us fear driving bikes or cars on this stretch but this girl seemed at ease while driving. It must have been her customary route as there were a few dried bristly wild growing plants too. I halted and found out about those twigs. She got down from the bicycle and told me that it was for fire wood. I recognised that she worked as a maid. I looked and nodded my head saying "school". She understood what I intended to know. She said studies and school were in her village but here she was a maid. A little ahead I saw the garbage being sorted and sold to other rag pickers. There were a few weird looking people too.

A youngster who had taken the responsibility was seated on the bags as he was computing the produce.

Garbage has indeed become a produce these days. Affluence has led to wastefulness with a lack of prudence. By now the little girl was far away. I was walking at a fast pace reflecting the proceeds. I reminisced my childhood when I fostered fear on being sent on errands in the evenings. I saw a few more youngsters go across the place. They spoke in hushed voices with terror transfixing them. Girls were escorted by their parents. Every one traversing the path was laden with trepidation but the little girl who carried those twigs knew no fear perhaps she was more concerned about the twigs for firewood than about herself to be aware of her loneliness to experience a fear while crossing the trail. It reminded me that

"Courage is not the absence of fear, but rather the judgement that something else is more important than fear." — Ambrose Redmoon

45

THE FILM SHOOT

"Just when the caterpillar thought the world was over,
it became a butterfly" Pinner Maddison Elyse

It was 8.30 on Thursday morning. The maid had begun mopping prompting my husband to move to the balcony to braze the air and lo behold he was flabbergasted to see lot of hubbub in the otherwise hushed premises of our housing block. He dragged me to the terrace even as we saw a cine film equipment vehicle unload the shooting equipment. I looked around to glimpse heads sneak a look through windows. People were in their porches wondering what next. We speculated as to who had given the consent as ours was in totality a residential complex. A few months ago when the workers from Aqua -tech had come for the standard maintenance of the water tank there had been a burglary in one of the flats. The watchman had been whisked away to the police station by two burly stern looking policemen and released in the afternoon. There was quick appointment of additional staff. There after every one was vigilant. As time passed by, to our delight we saw every spot of the campus being prepared for a Marathi film shoot. There was an auto brought along and many reflectors, lights, make up men artists, metallic chairs and many more. The entire campus was swiftly filled with people. Ladies scurried their hubbies to their workplaces and waited in the lawns for the shooting to begin. Most of the kids had been ushered to school. Young and the old were on the phone and on whats app to inform their near and dear ones about the film shoot displaying the importance of their property.

I was lucky as our flat opens on three sides helping me observe from all the corners. A few young ladies became a part of the shoot when they were given a tiny role of walking along the long path from the main gate. There were two lady director too. We kept waiting for the shoot to begin. I saw a little progress. I got geared up to go to the University as the Research committee wanted a few changes to be carried out. For a few days I was upset as it meant a whole lot of changes and a lot more work. The driver Mr. Salunke who had come to take me also enjoyed the shoot. I concluded my work and came back. The driver was now no longer interested as it was over and above lunch time. The cine directors were still shooting. I saw that the scene was to walk straight to the entrance of the 'E' block enclave. The man was dressed as a college boy and there was another young girl clad in denims. The director gave the clap as the boy walked to reach the place, followed by the girl. They said it was not satisfactory.

They directed him to walk on another path and then it went on many times. They measured,calculated, precised, focussed, reflected and were dejected till the one last time. By now I was terribly bored watching the identical scenes again and again but the actor seemed calm and poised. He kept doing his best.

At this moment I saw the man take a last route which was overflowing with the shade of the trees lining the paved firmament. It looked the best and of course the director was happy. They closed down for lunch. I gazed for a long time to realize that truly persistent people are successful as they nurture the PHD attitude as Rick Pitino says, "the poor, hungry, driven attitude". My research no longer seemed complicated as I grasped the changes were definitely to make me more resilient and triumphant.

"Success is almost totally dependent upon drive and persistence" Dennis Waitley

46

THE SAGA OF MY PAPAYA

"Plant seeds of happiness, hope, success, and love; it will all come back to you in abundance. This is the law of nature." — Steve Maraboli,

It looked insolently to the other side. It was no longer emerging straight; there was a characteristic bend half way through. Its body had begun to show a distinctive aridness, I wondered, were they wrinkles? It no longer bore the cheerful countenance that it had when I had first seen it. Its leaves no longer grew to the size they used to. There were a few baby leaves borne in the centre at the growing axis which were perhaps too young to apprehend the thorny situation. It was at daybreak when it dawned upon me that my papaya was perhaps suffering from Progeria a disease causing precocious maturity like Amitabh Bachchan in the film Paa. The only difference was Amitabh was suffering from a genetic disease while my papaya's was environmental. I sat at the doorway looking at it fondly as I reminisced the day we went to the Nursery near Royal Casa apartments. The Nursery of plants was a huge one with a central office all embedded and enraptured in plants which gave the place a Costa Rica like appearance. It was nearly six in the evening when we had entered the gates welcomed by a variety of hibiscus plants and other attractive plants. The nursery was covered with a green net for a few plants while the others were lying exposed. Probably for a few plants it was extra protection from UV radiations or the infrared radiations of the sun. I impetuously walked till the end of the freshly watered nursery and estimated whether some of these plants would be a delight for the cynosure's eye. I felt regal while selecting the timid plants who then seemed like the slaves who festooned the Greek homes.

I ultimately decided on a few plants in the flowering and fruiting categories. There were many Papaya plants reserved in plastic wrap and in mud pots. I cast a quick look to see this little plant which was the one I really treasured. I affectionately ran my fingers through its leaves just as we cuddle little children. I picked a miniature fruiting lemon plant too along with a few petunias and chrysanthemums. It was to begin a little terrace garden.

We bought long pots where two three plants could share space. But my Papaya and lemon got independent pots to flourish in. I glowed in pride as I transplanted the Papaya into its new living space and declared that the first Papaya fruit would go to my earnest maid. My maid works in homes due to her ardour for work. She is not a needy one but her genuineness and conscientiousness towards her occupation has always fascinated me. A Papaya would definitely be a reward. She looked at me fair-mindedly and said the plant needed space to spread its roots. Her expression fell on deaf years as nothing could tamper my zeal. I felt I could nurture it with all that money could procure and it would definitely be wheedled to grow and fruit.

Today as I looked at the frail papaya plant I felt I had sinned by captivating its capacities. Perhaps it would have grown better in the soil of any unkempt ground with bare essentials. I had given it everything needed for growing and blooming but somewhere I had not cared about the expected space it needed. It unexpectedly reminded me of children who are reared with all the care and conveniences to succeed but fail to do well perhaps because they never get their own space to exploit their potentials. In all probability their potentials were ruined by their overwhelming parents and occasionally by their teachers.

> Destiny is not a matter of chance; it is a matter of choice. It is not a thing to be waited for, it is a thing to be achieved." — William Jennings Bryan

47

An Inclination

Your success is defined by the altitude of your attitude and the magnitude of your aptitude.

The fishmonger pulled a fish and started cleaning its scales with a sharp knife. The noise diverted my notice. There were people surrounding her, perhaps to buy fish. The lady shook the motionless fish as she placed it on a stone and slit the head in one jerk. A quiver quavered me. It aggrieved me, prodding an unknown wound in me, pushing me into the past. I remember the incident vividly.

There were two white rats almost four inches big lying in chloroform in a glass bottle given by the lab attendee. Me and Suchi tugged them out and placed them on the solidified wax in the dissection tray. We had procured these from the school through the lab attendee. My sister had got married at Alapuzha in Kerala. Her wedding was appreciated by one and all as my father had achieved the feat of tagging my sister's life with my brother in law who was posted at Oman then. The appreciation was for the wealth associated. My sister felt it was excellent opportunity to live with us taking care of me and my siblings as my brother in law could visit India every three months on a month's leave.We all wept when we bid her adieu even though it was just for a month. On reaching back, I rushed to my friend suchitra's house to know the syllabus covered and the pre board exam schedule. We were in class twelfth and suchi was the closest of all friends. The moment Suchi saw me,she gave me a bear hug and stridently proclaimed how she missed me. She was open and demonstrative, though I felt the same, my feelings remained within me. I ostracized my brother in law for having seized away my sister in the months of January and February with the Board exams around the corner. Suchi slowly started listing the things I had missed. I came to know that the dissection of a specimen representing class Mammalia had been taught during Biology practicals and since the rats were expensive,no more practice would be given. I asked her whether the dirty black ones were used for dissection. She said they were given the beautiful white ones. She was confident of dissecting and I felt my world turning dark as I had missed the most scoring accomplishment in Biology. I looked at her helplessly. She said that she would think about it. A few days later we met the lab attender, had a talk and bought two rats for Rs 4 each. She said she would demonstrate it first and then I could understand and dissect the other rat. The rats were brought home. I am Gauda saraswat Brahmin while Suchi is an Iyengar Brahmin and so the question was at whose house. We decided to dissect it under the Guava tree in my house. I saw suchi perform the dissection explaining while feeling each part like our biology teacher, I followed her fearfully and as I ripped the body open to display all the systems,the digestive and the Urinogenital system. Soon a wave of confidence crept through me. I thanked Suchi as she had managed to bring me back into the examination mood. We planned a routine and began studying. We were sincere but never knew how to prepare for exam oriented studies. We thought logically and could speak on any topic in the world other than the terrorising effects of Physics.

On the the day we had the final Biology practicals we were given a flower to be dissected and a white rat. There were few other things to be spotted. I thanked God and of course Suchi silently as we performed the practicals. The bell rang signifying us to submit our papers. The External Examiner stopped ahead at my classmate Manga's table asking her about her rat. Manga my classmate told the external that she was a Brahmin by caste and in deeds too. She outrightly told the examiner that she could never kill a living organism. The specimens given are unconscious and every one of us kill it while dissecting. The examiners questioned her the reason for taking up Biology and her goal of turning into a doctor. She smiled sheepishly saying she would think about it.

Over the years when we had zoology practicals in our graduation, I detested dissecting frogs or prawns. The frogs were dirty, slippery with an abdomen filled with spawn. We killed animals of each category, we etched our name on the tiny sharks and spilled blood out of the leech's mouth before dissecting. I wrote the pre medical entrance twice. I was full of remorse on knowing that I hadn't cleared the medical entrance inspite of the fact that any scene involving blood would startle me and that I never had an aptitude for it. Years later me and Suchi grew into versatile teachers due to the gift of gab. Luckily dissections have been prohibited to sensitise students. Perhaps one should inspire children to choose a profession where their spirit lies rather than to prefer a profession to raise their admiration in the society.

48

AN ACTIVE RETIRED LIFE

Starting today, I need to forget what's gone, appreciate what still remains and look forward to what's coming next. Toni Nicolle (Inspirational Quotes)

There was a thoughtful stillness in the group. I could hear my loud footsteps which slowly faded as I slowed my pace, and subsequently I heard the wisest speaking in a drooling sound in Marathi. My curiosity made me glance at them. I saw a group of elderly men surrounding a man sitting on a bench near the man made lake. The sun was yet to rise but it was dawn,the tranquillity of the lake,the serene environment matched the poise of these gentlemen in their maturity. The members of the group varied in the age group of sixty to seventy. I recalled how they congregate early in the morning at the gate of the forest hills,Durga Tekdi. With the transformed pleasant weather, rousing and going for walks has become pleasurable, nevertheless the sun rises well past seven in the morning. A day begun well with an enjoyable fitness exercise well before a schedule no longer seems challenging for the enthusiasts and those who are passionate about their dynamism. Perhaps this is why people throng to parks and other health centres to be in the pink of health. Most of the Doctors and a few other professionals are regular for their walks at this time inspiring others to follow suit. Our family Doctor who has a malfunction in one of his legs is the first to complete his walk before his wife who is an anesthetist. We can see him waiting for his wife at the gate as he listens to music with a beaming smile. There are two old women who relax for a while on the paved firmament before retreating home at this time. Many a times I wonder at their punctuality and steadiness prevailing in their retreating years. We reach well before six and feel sheepish if it crosses quarter past six in the morning. There are youngsters who run throughout the walking area, there are adults,mothers and the elderly.

The silent group near the lake is a prominent group whose members are known to return back by seven. They love being kiddish playing football in one of the clearings near the temple. Their place of meeting and their silence intrigued me. They were aloof from the normal track, little away from the track which leads directly to the lawns. I had taken this course to reach back earlier than usual. They did not converse but their silence tortured me. I moved ahead to hear one gentleman speak about angioplasty and bypass surgery, a heart surgery. He was advising the alarmed elderly person seated on the bench that an angioplasty was safer than the bypass surgery.

The person seated was perhaps advised by the doctor. He seemed terrified and wished against hope that he should not have been in this state of torment. The others who were standing were advising, a few nurtured the fear whether they would have the same fate but there was one elderly person known to me, who had great strength within him. He is more than seventy three years old and has undergone a coronary bypass surgery but was back for his regular walks within twenty days. People say walking uphill is risky but this gentleman walks twice the track beating youngsters at this feat. He has only his wife for support with his children settled in America. He stood listening and looking at the others, it was as if the message was dominant, overriding and obvious to all others. They gathered themselves, changed the topic and as I left I could hear their normal laughter and chatter. Perhaps they had resolved to face the ups and downs of life with courage to say "Try me" rather than "Why me". Probably the Republic day celebrations must have helped them resolve to lead Indians to a fitter India by being role models or they must have seeded inspiration to break the shackles of panic and apprehension by leading an active retired life.What ever was the reason it was an insight to advance in life. Wishing all the readers a very Happy Republic Day.

49

STRENGTH OR WEAKNESS

> People grow old only by deserting their ideals and outgrowing the consciousness of their youth. Years wrinkle the skin but to give up enthusiasm wrinkles the soul.......Dr. L.F.Phelan

The sweetmeat proprietor stood in the corner, his thoughts focussed towards a young lad who sat on the manager's chair. There were helpers who were busy stuffing Balushahi, an Indian confectionery in packets. The shop was owned by the sweetmeat retailer who is a Balushahi specialist. I came to know this through the printed wrap of the packet in which they pack the savouries. The shop was crammed with a variety of snacks, hot and sweet. There were sweetmeats being made. A few were lying open to cool down. It was evening and the shop was brimming with people. We picked our favourite Ding laddoo which is particularly healthy for winters as it has the gum of plants, a kind of resin, as we stood near the counter. I was looking for telltale signs to know who the young man was. He resembled the owner but seemed studious with his spectacles and I could corroborate it from the owner's loving smile. I looked at the proprietor who is not more than fifty. I smiled back as we were regular customers. He wanted me to know that the young man was his son. I softly told him that it was his cheerful countenance and his appeal which attracted all of us to his shop. I recalled the day when the owner began his career outside the shop a decade back. He had very little money and so the savouries were made on orders. People distrusted his appearance and the pumping stove but he and his wife were constant companions never giving up. He had the advantage of hawking his goods at the busiest spot'. Slowly he started getting generous orders. As time stirred on, he moved into the shop, and introduced a few well known packed savouries for the people who believed in nitrogen packed savouries and sweets like laddoo, anarasa, karaunji for Diwali and other festivals. His specialisation, the Balushahi won him customers from far and near. He grew busier with time and so did the area with the whole locale filled with Bhel puri vendors, soda, fruit juice vendors and not to forget the ice cream shops. Dilli swad a fast food chain opened its outlet but the sweetmeat wholesaler had turned into an enterprising business man growing leaps and bounds with Pune turning into an IT sector. Hinjewadi the IT park brought many professionals to the city soaring the property prices turning the place into a crowded one. Being professionals with a good pay packet gave way for the sweetmeat shop to grow. He employed assistants and handed over the art to his helpers.

He would now be seen relaxing while his helpers cooked. His shop still had the human touch and the things were made out of the best ingredients in the market. He now had time to talk to the customers. What attracted us was his smile and his humility. But today as he cast a conceited look at the youngster whom I had never seen anywhere near the shop earlier made me a little apprehensive about the future. The boy did have his father's looks but he seemed more realistic. He was committed in collecting money,adding and subtracting profits. Somewhere I felt the unassuming nature which attracted us to the shop was missing.

It reminded me of an old lady bent with age who prefers sitting at her roadside stall rather than handing it to her children, perhaps death would only retire her. I could recollected another young lady pushing her vegetable cart to the market square reminding me that retirement or growing old should be the point when one is powerless of managing affairs rather than bequeathing the excruciatingly brought up entrepreneurship to children who have never seen your great effort to comprehend your voyage.

You are as old as you doubt, your fear, your despair. Keep your self confidence young. keep your hope young.............. Dr. L.F.Phelan

50

SHIFTING BRILLIANCE

Discipline trains the tremendously important habit of mind control and positive thinking- Robin Sharma

He gazed intently oblivious of his surroundings. He seemed proud of his accomplishment, and I felt the pride turning into arrogance as we glanced curiously, perhaps there were a few appreciating looks too. He and his sister were sitting on a small couch in a corner of a nondescript beauty parlour just beyond our lane. He was about nine years old and his sister must have been eight years old. They were in their school uniforms which had the school emblem on the shirt and on their tie. Their uniform was a combination of shades of sky blue and dark blue. Their school bags were lying on the floor near the couch. The boy was peering deeply into the touch screen mobile while the girl kept glancing around prying to know more. Both were fair and well built for their age. They seemed intelligent and responded well to my questions but the boy never looked up. His attention was painstakingly focussed on the mobile. Their mother was a tall, well built dark lady who was anxious about her growing years and kept probing the beautician for therapies regarding pigmentation, dark circles around her eyes.

The beautician resorted to marketing tactics and responded by saying that the lady needed a good facial of Shehnaaz or Oriflamme costing above two thousand rupees to lose the dark circles below her eyes and a few sitting to overcome the pigmentation. It was around six in the evening but these little kids in their school uniforms and bags had accompanied their mother skipping their play time. Perhaps they had been ushered here directly from the school but the lady seemed very familiar and recognisable which meant they lived nearby. The lady appeared happy with the beautician's deductions and therapy as she promised to begin these at the earliest. Growing years bewilder women and many are unable to accept it gracefully. The little girl now looked around at all the lipsticks, mirrors and pictures hung. Perhaps she wished to grow fast like her beautiful mother to attempt all these solutions. I could not stop myself from talking to the children and so asked the boy whether he was comfortable with a touch screen mobile. The mother answered promptly saying that the boy was gifted and actually felt at home operating a computer and the mobile. I felt the pleasure and pride in the answer but all parents are proud of their children.

I remembered one of my husband's colleague whose son was versatile operating the computer at the age of five.

The long hours in front of the computer had endowed the boy with thick glass spectacles. I recalled another friend of mine who bought a video game for her daughter motivating her to improve her score each day saying it improved the concentration power with consistent gazing. I saw the concentration of this boy was also great. I recalled my childhood days when my mother would send us to the playground in the evenings. We would play, jump and enjoy it every moment. It improved our concentration power because it helped us forget everything else in the sheer bliss of working out a sound body. I felt this mother would have appeared better had she walked and let her children play in the evening rather than bringing them to a beauty parlour exploiting their innocence. These children were losing their virtuousness in the environment the mother exposed subtly as they were on the threshold of adolescence. I reminisced the workshop of Manahshakti Kendra from Lonavala which taught us never to coax a child to achieve but to expose the child to the environment which would cleverly enthuse that which you wanted your children to be. I recalled the books and magazines brought from the libraries which helped me in my growing years. I recollected how my mother learnt reading Tamil within a few days to share Tamil magazines with her friend. She was a voracious reader, the first one to pick the weekly and fortnightly magazines from the daily circulating library which helped us imbibe the habit of reading. Children are a visual rendering of their parents in all likeness. These days reading has become a rare trait and with mother's equipping children with mobiles and computers it may turn into a extinct trait. There is nothing genius in being hooked to a PC or mobile but the self discipline of using it judiciously by debating it with reading and playing will turn one into a true whiz kid.

'What we do upon some great occasion will probably depend upon what we already are; and what we are will be the result of previous years of self discipline' H.P.Liddon

51

An identity

"And yet she was leaving the world as a woman who had love and been loved back. she was leaving it as a friend, a companion, a guardian, a mother, a person of consequence at last." — Khaled Hosseini

She held the round board with a stand displaying 'Stop' sign,with her other hand she directed where we had to stop. We wondered whether we were in the wrong place as our minds were accustomed to a man stopping us rather than lady, but she stood there bearing a mature demeanour as we halted where she had directed us to. We have been to this fuel filling station commonly known as the petrol pump for the past eleven years. Each time we visited we found something new here. In the initial years this was the best petrol pump as the other one at Nigdi was always crowded. With the growth in the infra structure of the place and the population many petrol pumps and CNG centers have mushroomed up. This had a super bazaar too for a few years. My son was a little boy and so we would rush in to amuse him when the wait would be long. I learnt the art of cooking Manchurian from a young girl who managed this super bazaar. My son adored me for mastering this art and so this place is very close to my heart. Since the time a new petrol pump appeared close to home our visits here are infrequent. The girl was a young girl probably in her early twenties. She was neatly clad in a salwar kameez with her dupatta pinned. She had no expressions on her face but seemed confident. She seemed educated, a little disinterested in the job. She left her place came near us to enquire the amount for which we wished fill fuel. She then slowly rolled the meter to zero and asked me to look at the amount as she filled petrol. I was so thrilled that I hopped out to click a photograph. I smiled and appreciated her on her new job. I felt I could make her recognise her efforts. She now seemed happier and thanked me in English with a mam attached. She then dipped the wiper in diesel and swiped the glass as we left.

This brought to mind the dumping ground in Pradhikaran near the excise office and the PCMC lawn tennis ground, where the garbage transporting trucks are parked. Early morning at seven I have seen women rush to take their Garbage truck to collect garbage and transport it to this place. It was sheer delight watching women drive these vehicles.

The newly built skeleton of the building brought about memories of a women sieving sand for concrete while the men looked on. I was also reminded of the young lady who was skipping under the shade of a tree on a winter morning before her family roused outside a building site. Perhaps she was taking care of her health to serve her family and to work at the site.

The daily news displayed the women from remote Rajasthan learning to make a solar circuit as a solution to overcome the electricity problem. The enthusiasm had lead this old lady to begin her studies too. Then there was this young girl who worked as a maid in my sister's house as she continued her studies and now works for a call center. She found a role model in my sister and aims to join the reserve bank. There are young and old women working long hours, reaching home late but still not neglecting the families.

There are women drivers, pilots, directors and many more successful ladies. It reminded me of my mother speaking about an uniqueness, an individuality or an identity for everyone. She wanted to work but the responsibility of four kids never left time. With the rolling years my father rose on the corporal ladder and was posted at Delhi on a special mission for which he was awarded, but my mother stayed back to take care of our studies. She began feeling the loneliness and felt dejected many a times for the fact that she did not have an identity despite the fact that our individualities were a gift of her endowment. She voiced her thoughts saying that any vocation lends an identity to appreciate that one did not let life go by as stones and trees. It may be a service to the society or money for home, it could be service for the family, a job does wonders in enhancing the potentials and turning life into a momentous one conferring uniqueness.

"The best way to find yourself is to lose yourself in the service of others." — Mahatma Gandhi

52

AN INVESTMENT

A P J Kalam says when people in their later years look back with bewilderment and regret, they will not be able to accept the choices made. They will wish for another chance. A meaningful old age comes out of a meaningful life.

I have been a teacher for more than two decades and have worked in various schools at Mumbai,Hyderabad and Pune. I learnt that the art of teaching was rampant in my blood genetically as my father was also one for a short time. Perhaps it was the respect for the profession by my family which helped me understand the nobleness of the endeavour. In our profession though we reek in values in children,teachers envy each other for creativity, a gain in higher position like corporate without accepting what facilitating knowledge means to this profession, mostly challenging their values.

In the year 2005, I joined the school run by Chinchwad Malayalee Samaj and here I met my friend. Duly we understood that we shared the same interests of art, music,teaching and many other things. She happens to be many years younger than me but is mature beyond my years in perception and behaviour. She was the one who kindled a spark in me to pursue my studies for which I will be ever grateful. As my husband works for a transferable job I weaned out and joined the Army School and this was nearer to the Kendriya Vidyalaya where my son studied. This distance never perturbed our friendship as we met regularly during our evening walks. Her involvement in her school is total and her loyalty can never be questioned. She is a Gandhian in deeds with minimum needs and has principles which have influenced me at all times. When we are on walks we pluck petunias and discuss a still life drawing or sing songs which could be used in our schools or converse about our students for betterment rather than for case studies.

One of those summer holidays she called me up excitedly and said she needed to share a good news and I consented to meet her. On reaching our normal meeting place we parked our scooters and began walking. She told me "do you know I have adopted two kids from the orphanage (name withheld) A boy and a girl who are around five and seven years old". She explained that she would be shouldering their financial responsibilities. Many a times teachers aren't paid as corporate employees and taking up such a dependability for a teacher is financially a big constraint chiefly when the permanency of a job is not identified. I had nothing but admiration for her as I have heard people invest in buying homes but a mere school teacher had invested in the future of India. I think we all need to make our own lives meaningful too perhaps bonding with vision India.